"Where's Tammy?"

"Uh, she had a headache," Tessa sputtered. "It's one of her bad ones, Alex. A migraine."

"Yeah?" His mouth twisted cynically. "A migraine, huh."

"Look," Tessa said defensively, "Tammy didn't mean to get sick . . . "

"Sick," he repeated incredulously. "You really think she's got a headache?"

He drummed his fingers lightly against the tall glass in front of him. "I didn't expect her to come. I mean, I'm getting used to her flaking out at the last minute. Especially when we'd planned to go somewhere where they check ID before bringing you a glass of wine . . . "

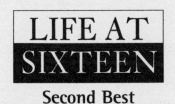

Second Best

LIFE AT SIXTEEN

Second Best

Cheryl Lanham

BERKLEY BOOKS, NEW YORK

SECOND BEST

A Berkley Book / published by arrangement with
the author

PRINTING HISTORY
Berkley edition / September 1997

The Putnam Berkley World Wide Web site address is
http://www.berkley.com

ISBN: 0-425-15545-5

BERKLEY®
Berkley Books are published by The Berkley Publishing Group,
200 Madison Avenue, New York, New York 10016, a member of
Penguin Putnam Inc.
BERKLEY and the "B" design
are trademarks belonging to Berkley Publishing Corporation.

PRINTED IN THE UNITED STATES OF AMERICA

10 9 8 7 6 5 4 3 2 1

LIFE AT SIXTEEN

SIXTEEN

Second Best

CHAPTER
ONE

June 19

Dear Diary,
  I'm not going to let them get away with this!
What do they think I am, a sack of spuds? Well,
maybe they can make me go to Lansdale, but they
can't make me like it. Just because she finally
took it into her head that she wants to meet me,
doesn't mean I have to make things easy for her.
Or them.

Tessa Prescott looked at the words she'd just written and dropped her pencil in disgust. It immediately rolled off the tray and onto the floor of the
plane, where it probably proceeded to roll all the
way back to the bathrooms. Tessa didn't much
care. She didn't want to be on a plane anyway and
she sure as heck didn't want to be on her way to
Santa Barbara.

She made a face and then quickly glanced at the seats across the aisle, hoping that no one had noticed. But the businessman sitting there had his nose buried in a magazine and the blonde woman next to him was still sound asleep.

What was she going to do? Why had her parents done this to her? It didn't make any sense. Tessa didn't want to meet her birth mother. Except for being mildly curious about the woman, she'd never expressed any desire to meet her mother or this sister she had.

The flight attendant's smooth voice cut into Tessa's thoughts. "Would you like something to drink?"

"Uh, no thanks," she answered. "I'm fine." That was a lie. Her stomach was so tied in knots she couldn't choke down anything. She was miserable. How could they have done this to her?

Tessa slowly closed her diary and pushed the tray into the upright position. They'd be landing soon. Los Angeles to Santa Barbara wasn't that long a flight. In a few minutes she'd be face-to-face with the woman who'd given her away. She swallowed nervously and told herself to get a grip. Maybe it wouldn't be so bad. Maybe her parents were right and meeting her biological mother and sister would be a good thing.

Maybe she'd sprout wings and fly.

She closed her eyes and leaned back in the seat. She couldn't believe her life had gone down the tubes so fast. Just last week she was graduating from South Hollywood High; Dad, of course, taping the entire graduation ceremony. Tessa smiled in spite of her misery. Typical for her father to tape not only her getting her diploma, but the entire ceremony. She wasn't even embarrassed by his excesses anymore. Once he'd showed up for one of her volleyball matches with a whole camera crew. A bunch of guys who owed him a big favor. She'd almost died of humiliation. But her dad hadn't cared. He'd just taped away, grinning with pride and not caring that Tessa's team got their butts whipped good. Her father, Chuck Prescott, was a well-respected second-unit director in movies and television; her mother, Lorna Prescott, a second-lead character actress. But despite their flashy occupations, they were good parents. Ridiculously overprotective, of course. But Tessa knew they loved her. So how could they do this to her?

She opened her eyes and stared out the window at the brown hills and valleys of the coastal range. She didn't believe for one minute what they'd told her last week, that they were sending her to stay with her birth mother for her own good. What was good about meeting someone who had dumped you? Darn, why couldn't her adoption have been one of those cloaked-in-secrecy-with-the-records-forever-sealed kind. But no, her parents had actually known the name of her biological mother, had actually kept in touch through one of those organizations for adoptee rights. Just her luck, her parents had wanted to make sure she could contact her biological relatives if she wanted to. Tessa snorted faintly at the idea. And she certainly didn't buy that number that they didn't want her staying alone in the family home in the Hollywood Hills all summer. Her father and mother were going to Mexico, shooting a film together near Acapulco.

Until last week, Tessa had planned to have a fabulous summer. For once, she wouldn't have been right under Mommy and Daddy's noses. For goodness' sake, she was seventeen. If life had gone according to her plan, she'd have spent the summer waiting tables a few hours a week at Maxie's Eats and the rest of the time she'd be sunning herself on the beach or strolling the malls with her friends.

Tessa straightened her spine and sat up in her seat. Well, she decided angrily, she wasn't going to make it easy on them. Not on her parents or on the woman who'd given birth to her. If they wanted to ruin her life by sending her to some cow town named Lansdale just because her parents thought it would be good for her, then they'd just have to pay the price. She'd be sullen, silent, and cranky. She'd make them all sorry for ruining her summer. That would teach them.

But as quickly as it had come, the idea lost its appeal. She slumped back in her seat. The truth was, she wasn't much good at making things tough on people. It was impossible for her not to talk, and sulking was such a stupid thing to do that she didn't think she could keep it up for a single day, let alone an entire summer. Darn. She had far too much of a conscience to be deliberately mean to people. That was her parents' fault, too.

Even her friends razzed her about it. Melanie had

told her only last week, when they were at the mall blowing Melanie's allowance, that Tessa was the only person she'd ever met who'd gotten all the way through high school without cheating on a test, lying to her parents, smoking a joint, or drinking a beer.

Tessa was secretly proud of herself. It made her sound like a blatant nonconformist. And compared with most of the kids at South Hollywood High, she was. She wished she could add cigarettes to the list of things she'd never done, but when she was fourteen she and Melanie had swiped a pack of Benson & Hedges and made themselves sick in Melanie's pool house. She'd gotten caught, of course. Her mother had taken one sniff of her clothes and known. That little escapade had earned her more than a lecture. Her parents hadn't grounded her—oh no, that would have been too normal. Instead, her dad got hold of some slides from the studio archives and made her sit through a really gross evening looking at the lungs of smokers. It had worked, though; after seeing those horrible slides, Tessa'd never again been tempted to smoke.

"Please return all trays to the upright position and fasten your seat belts. We're beginning our descent to the Santa Barbara Airport."

The announcement sent Tessa's stomach all the way to her toes. Her hands shook as she fumbled with her seat belt. "Get a grip," she muttered fiercely to herself. "You're acting like a baby."

"Did you say something, miss?" the silver-haired man in the seat across the aisle asked.

"Uh, no, I was just talking to myself." That was another habit she'd better be careful about. Her parents were used to it, but who knew how the Mercers would react. They might call the men with the butterfly nets if they caught her wandering around their house muttering.

The plane touched down and bumped along the runway. Tessa took long, deep breaths, hoping to calm her nerves. When the flight attendants opened the doors, she stayed seated.

Her birth mother had waited almost seventeen years to want to see her, she could wait a few minutes more.

As the other passengers filed off the plane Tessa reached in her handbag and pulled out her compact. Checking her reflection in the mirror, she thought she looked okay. Her long hair, pulled back in a ponytail, was still safely anchored in the bright red scrunchy that matched the tunic top she had on. Her makeup, light and natural, just like her mom had taught her, hadn't worn off, and as far as she could tell, no new zits had popped out on her nose as a result of being so nervous she could scream. As she stood up she saw one of the male flight attendants staring at her approvingly. Tessa didn't let it go to her head. She knew she was pretty. Petite and dark-haired, she made the most of her assets. But as her mother often said, "Pretty on the outside isn't nearly as good as pretty on the inside." Strange advice, considering her mother's occupation.

Slinging her weekend bag out of the overhead luggage compartment, she took one long, last deep breath and slowly started down the aisle. As she reached the door of the plane she was just petty enough to hope that her sister, the one her mother had kept, was fat as a pig and had zits as big as volcanoes.

Tessa's heart pounded like a jackhammer as she stepped into the terminal. She glanced around the uncrowded space, realizing that she had no idea what the Mercers would look like. How was she supposed to find them? Skimming the few people standing around, she spotted a group of three people huddled together at the end of the walkway. Her jaw dropped.

For a moment she thought she was seeing things. Then she realized that the girl with her face had short hair. But that was the only difference between them. Her sister. It had to be.

The girl spotted Tessa, poked the woman standing next to her in the ribs, and the group started forward. Tessa couldn't take her eyes off the girl. It was weird, it was bizarre, it was like watching herself in a mirror but knowing the mirror was warped.

"Hello, you must be Tessa."

Tessa dragged her gaze away from the girl to stare in the direction of the voice. The woman smiling at her had short dark hair, perfectly cut and curled, a thin face with exquisite makeup, and brown, teary eyes. "Yeah, I, uh, mean, yes." Tessa awkwardly extended her hand. "I'm Tessa Prescott."

"I'm . . ." The woman laughed self-consciously. "Well, you know who I am. Please call me Doreen." She turned to the tall, silver-haired man next to her. "This is my husband, Harold Mercer and . . ."

"I'm Tammy," the girl interrupted. Like Tessa, she was staring. "Your twin."

"Twin?" Tessa shook her head, more stunned than she'd ever been in her life. "That explains why we look so much alike."

Tammy laughed. "Didn't you guess? Except for our hair, I'd say we were about as alike as two peas in a pod. Not that I've ever seen a pea in a pod, but it's a good expression. You didn't know we were twins?"

Tessa shook her head. "No . . . uh, I didn't." She felt a bit foolish, like she was the last one to get a joke.

"Come along, then," Harold said as he glanced at his watch and favored the girls with a brief smile. "I've got a meeting tonight after dinner and I'd like to go over my report before we eat."

The drive from the airport to Lansdale was short, and Tessa was too stunned to notice much of the town. The Mercers didn't talk much. Doreen sat in the front seat of the luxurious sedan, her eyes straight ahead and her spine as stiff as a poker. Except for perfunctory "how was the flight?" kinds of questions, she didn't say much.

Tessa thought she was either as cold as a glacier or too nervous to come up with any interesting small talk.

Harold concentrated on his driving. He didn't say anything either, and Tammy seemed too busy staring at Tessa to bother with conversation.

All in all, it was one of the longest rides of Tessa's life. She didn't know what to make of the situation. What were you supposed to say to a woman who'd given you away? What kind of questions did you ask a twin you didn't know you had? She still couldn't believe she had a twin sister and that no one had bothered to tell her.

A twin.

How could the woman who sat so calmly in the front seat have separated twins? How *could* she?

The awkward ride finally ended when Harold pulled into the driveway of a huge, two-story home in a swanky residential area. Tessa tried not to stare. Although she wasn't exactly from a deprived background, this place made her parents' modest three-bedroom home look like a shack.

"Wow," Tessa murmured as they got out of the car. "It sure is big." The house was painted a pale cream and had red tiles on the roof. A balcony overlooked the three-car garage and the walkway leading to the walled entrance was paved with huge slabs of brick-colored Mexican tile.

Tammy shrugged. "It's only five bedrooms and four baths. There's a pool in the back, of course. And a Jacuzzi. But it's nothing special." She led the way into an enclosed courtyard and up to a set of double oak doors. "Come on in, I'll take you up to your room."

"Shouldn't we help with the luggage?" Tessa asked.

"Harold will get it," Tammy answered, opening the door and stepping inside.

Tessa tried not to gape, but it was impossible. The interior of the house was even more impressive than the exterior. A twinkling chandelier hung from the ceiling directly in front of the staircase. Thick blue carpeting led off the parquet-floored foyer into a sunken living room to her left. To her right, she could see a family room with a fireplace and beyond that a formal dining room.

"Your room's right next to mine," Tammy said as she started up the staircase.

Tessa stifled a pang of disappointment as she followed her sister. Since learning her sibling was a twin, she'd hoped they'd share a room.

"We're at this end of the house." Tammy turned as she got to the top of the stairs. She pointed down the thickly carpeted hall. "There's two guest rooms and the master suite down there."

Tessa thought the hall looked a mile long. Apparently, Harold and Doreen didn't want to be bothered with noisy teenagers. Their daughter's room was as far from theirs as possible.

Tammy opened a door and waved Tessa inside. Tessa gasped. The room was straight out of a fairy tale, with a double bed with a white lace canopy in one corner, sheer lace curtains at the window, a delicate cream-colored dressing table, lace-covered stool, and matching armoire. "It's beautiful," she murmured.

Tammy shrugged. "She decorated it herself. She likes doing stuff like that. The bathroom's over there." She pointed to a door next to the armoire. "You've got a few minutes before dinner. Why don't you wash your face or freshen up or something?"

With that, Tammy left. Tessa stared around her, wondering what to do. Was she supposed to hide out up here till someone came and got her for dinner? When *was* dinner anyway? "Oh, to heck with it," she mumbled. She went into the bathroom, which turned out to be as opulent as the bedroom, and washed her hands. When she came out, her luggage was sitting at the foot of her bed.

"What are your favorite subjects in school?" Doreen asked. They were seated around the dining table like the points on a compass. Harold and Doreen were at east and west, Tammy and Tessa at north and south. Tessa thought this was the longest meal she'd ever had.

"I like history the best," she murmured. "English literature is my second favorite."

"History, huh?" Harold shook his head. "Literature. Not really very practical subjects, are they?"

Tessa started to reply, but Tammy interrupted. "What do you think kids in high school ought to study—business?"

"Wouldn't do them any harm," Harold replied.

He looked at his watch. "Give kids a solid under-standing of business, that's what I say. Teach them what really runs this world."

"You mean money," Tammy said.

"There's nothing wrong with money, young lady." Harold shook his fork at her.

Doreen interrupted. "I saw your, er, mother on television the other day," she said to Tessa. "She's a lovely woman."

"And a good actress, too," Tessa said firmly. For some reason, it was important to her that this woman understand that Lorna Prescott wasn't just a pretty face. She was her mom and Tessa suddenly realized she was really proud of her. She was a good actress, she'd spent years perfecting her craft and building a professional reputation. Lorna would never be a superstar or a big lead, but she was a terrific character actress. She was a good mom, too. Tessa wished she were with her now. Anything, even listening to one of Lorna's lectures, would be better than sitting around this dinner table trying to choke down roast beef and mashed po-tatoes with a bunch of strangers. Again, she won-dered how her parents could have done this to her.

"Hollywood people." Harold shook his head again. "Not a very stable environment for raising a child. All those divorces, drugs. Drinking." He looked at his watch again.

Tessa was annoyed at these remarks. "It's as stable as any other environment," she declared. "My parents don't drink and they don't do drugs either." The truth was, her parents were rabid on both subjects. They'd seen firsthand the damage booze and drugs could do. Tessa couldn't remember the last time she'd seen either of them even take a sip of wine. For Hollywood types, they were woefully straight.

"I'm sure that Harold didn't mean to imply anything," Doreen interjected smoothly. "He was merely making a general observation."

Harold smiled briefly, shoved his plate away, and stood up. "I've got to get to that meeting," he announced. "Sorry I can't be here this evening, but this is important."

"Don't apologize, Harold." Doreen also stood up. "I'm sure Tessa understands that our life can't come to a complete halt just because she's visiting with us." She gave Tessa a quick smile. "I've got a meeting, too."

"Tonight?" Tammy asked.

"I'm afraid so, dear." Doreen smoothed her skirt. "There's been a terrible mix-up over the dates for the charity dance and the golf tournament. The board's called an emergency meeting to figure out what to do. Besides, this will give you two the chance to get to know each other. We'll talk tomorrow."

Tessa told herself she was relieved that this dreadful meal was over, but deep inside, she was hurt. Her first night here and her birth mother was going out.

As soon as her parents had left the dining room, Tammy stood up. "Let's go up to my room and talk."

"Shouldn't we clear the table?" Tessa hadn't walked away from a dirty table since she was seven and could carry a dish without dropping it.

"The maid will do it. She comes in at six."

Upstairs, Tessa was surprised to see that Tammy's room, while larger than hers, was actually quite ordinary. The walls were painted a pale yellow with white trim along the door frames. There was a white chenille spread on the double bed, dark green carpeting, and plain white curtains at the windows. Opposite the bed was a mini–entertainment center, with a television, VCR, and stereo. To the left of that was a double oak dresser and dressing table with a wooden stool. A couple of green velvet ballon-backed chairs flanked the entertainment center.

Seeing her sister's surprised face, Tammy laughed. "It used to look like something out of a fairy-tale book, but I redecorated last year. I couldn't stand staring at all that lace. Doreen had a fit."

"Doreen? You call your mother by her first name?" Tessa settled down on Tammy's bed. She watched her sister slip a CD in the stereo.

"Not to her face," Tammy replied. "With Doreen I've learned it's easier to go along with her pretenses. She likes to pretend she's supermom. Do you like Hootie and the Blowfish?"

"Yeah, sure." Tessa wondered what Tammy meant about her mother's "pretenses," but this didn't seem like a good time to ask. Maybe later this summer she'd figure out what was going on around here. Right now she just felt weird. On the one hand, she was curious to learn about her sister, and on the other, she felt like she'd been dropped on some kind of alien planet. This house wasn't at all like hers. If the situation had been reversed, and Tammy had come to visit her, her parents would have not only been home, they'd have made darned sure that their guest was entertained, fed, watered, and generally given the starring role.

Tammy hit the play button and then dropped down onto the bed next to Tessa. "So, tell me about yourself."

"There's nothing much to tell." Tessa shrugged. "I went to school, did okay, and graduated."

"Do you have a boyfriend?"

Tessa laughed. "I've dated a few guys, but nothing serious. My parents were pretty strict." Strict wasn't exactly the right word. They'd been ridiculous. The few guys that had shown up to take Tessa out had gotten the third degree from her dad. He was convinced that every male that came within two feet of her was either a serial killer or a demented rapist. Well, maybe he hadn't been that bad, but dating hadn't been easy, either.

"Mine aren't." Tammy made a face. "What kind of grades did you get."

Tessa shrugged. "Pretty good."

"What was your GPA?"

"Four-point-0." Tessa couldn't keep the pride out of her voice.

Tammy's dark brown eyes widened. "Wow, straight A's, that's a little better than 'pretty good.'

I only ended up with a two-point-five. I thought Harold was going to have a cow when he saw my final grades. They were hoping to pack me off to one of those snobby women's colleges back east, but now they're stuck with me for another two years. I'm going to go to the local junior college. Where are you going?''

"To the local junior college,'' Tessa admitted. "My parents don't have a lot of money. I mean, they make a lot when they work, the money's real good. But the entertainment industry is really competitive, and sometimes it's tough—jobs are hard to come by. Not that we're poor or anything,'' she added quickly.

"But with grades like that, don't you want to go to a good school?''

"There are plenty of good schools close to home and I might as well get my first two years as cheaply as I can.'' Tessa deliberately kept her voice neutral to hide the disappointment she'd felt when it had dawned on her that her folks really didn't have the money to send her to UCLA. It wasn't their fault; they'd saved for years for her education. But two years ago, they'd lost half their house in an earthquake, and despite being insured, they'd had to use their savings to rebuild.

She'd overheard her parents talking about getting a second mortgage to pay for Tessa's college tuition and she hated that idea. So she had told them she wanted to live at home and go to the local JC.

"Your parents liked the idea?'' Tammy was incredulous. "They want you to live at home for another two years?"

"Sure, that's what most of my friends are doing."

"Well, lucky you." Tammy yawned and changed the subject. "You didn't know we were twins, did you? I could tell by your expression when you got off the plane and saw me." She laughed.

"No." Tessa looked down at the bedspread. "Mom didn't tell me that."

"Me either. I mean, they didn't tell me till we were at the airport," Tammy said. "I was really pissed, too. I mean, we're identical twins and they didn't say a word."

"Identical?"

"Sure, couldn't you tell?" She jumped to her feet and pointed at the mirror over the bureau. "Take a look. Except for our hair, we're so much alike I don't think our own mothers could tell us apart."

Tessa didn't think the resemblance was that close. She had the feeling that Lorna could spot her in a roomful of clones. But she and Tammy *were* alike, nevertheless. They shared the same straight nose and high cheekbones, the same rounded chin and forehead. The same color hair.

"We *are* alike," Tessa murmured. It gave her an odd feeling, like something had been missing all of her life but she hadn't noticed because she didn't know it existed. Resentment, hot and fierce, shot through her. Twins. Identical. And they'd been separated for seventeen years.

Still watching their reflections, Tammy suddenly grinned. "Maybe I'll buy a wig. We could pull some really good stunts, you know. No one around here knows about you."

Tessa thought it sounded like the lamest idea she'd ever heard. She hated practical jokes, but she didn't want to annoy her sister. "Yeah." She smiled halfheartedly. "That's a good idea."

In the distance, she heard a phone ring and glanced at the phone beside Tammy's bed.

Tammy saw her confusion and explained. "That's my private line; that's why it's not ringing in here. The other phone is for the family. Hang on a minute, I'll grab the extension in your room. It's probably one of Doreen's friends." She rushed off, leaving the door open.

A few moments later Tammy called, "It's for you. I think it's long distance."

Tessa hurried into her room and took the phone. "It's probably Mom or Dad."

Sure enough, her mother's voice came on the line. "Hi, honey."

"Hi, Mom." The line crackled in Tessa's ear. Phone connections to Mexico weren't the best.

"I just wanted to make sure you arrived okay," Lorna said. Then her voice broke as she said something else.

"I can barely hear you," Tessa said. "But I got here fine."

"Good. You've got the number here at the hotel?"

Tessa rolled her eyes. "Yes, Mom. You put it in my purse, in my jeans, *and* in my suitcase." She was surprised they hadn't stapled it to her nose. "I know how to get hold of you."

"What, honey? I can't hear you real well. Oh, here comes your dad; he wants to say hello."

"Mom, Mom!" Tessa called before her mom put her dad on the line. There were a few questions she wanted to ask and it would be easier to worm the information out of her mother than her father.

Chuck Prescott's deep voice came on the line. "Hi, sweetheart. You got there okay?"

"Yeah, Dad, everything was just fine. How are you and Mom doing?"

"What? I can barely hear you, honey." More static.

"I said, how are things going?"

"Darn, honey, I can't hear a word you're . . . we'll call again tomorrow . . . better line . . . love."

The phone went dead in her hand. Tessa slowly put it down and went back to Tammy's room.

"That was fast," Tammy commented.

"It was a bad connection. They'll call again tomorrow." Knowing her parents, they'd probably call every day to make sure Tessa was taking her vitamins and getting enough sleep. Much as she loved them, they were a real pain sometimes.

"Did you ask them why they hadn't told you?" Tammy asked. "I mean about us being identical twins."

"No, I didn't get a chance." Tessa shrugged. "Besides, maybe they didn't know."

Tammy snorted. "They knew all right. They just didn't bother to say anything. Just like mine. Of course it's no wonder that Doreen didn't say anything to me. Half the time I think she forgets she's even got a daughter. Hey." She smiled suddenly. "Are you thirsty?"

"Sure." Not for the first time Tessa wondered at Tammy's abrupt changes of subject. Maybe Tammy wasn't as blasé about this whole business of being separated twins as she pretended to me.

"Good, so am I." She got off the bed and walked to the closet. Throwing open the door, she reached inside and pulled out a pair of black velvet boots.

"You've got sodas stashed in your closet?" Tessa asked.

Tammy reached into the boot. "Who said anything about soda?" She turned and held up a bottle. "I've got something here that'll give us a buzz a lot faster than sugar or caffeine."

Tessa didn't doubt that for a moment.

Tammy was holding a bottle of wine.

CHAPTER
TWO

June 20

Dear Diary,
You won't believe what happened last night. I can
barely believe it myself. I'm not sure how much
of this I should actually write down. I mean, I
don't want to get anyone in trouble or anything,
but who knows what kind of snoops there might
be in this house? It's not like I'm home, you know.
One thing I'll say for Mom and Dad, I could leave
you lying around open and they wouldn't have
violated my privacy.

Tessa stared at the words she'd just written and
made a face. She was sitting up in her bed, diary
on her lap. The sun was shining through the white
lace curtains, the house was quiet as a church, and
she couldn't decide what to do. It wasn't that she
thought that Doreen or Harold would actually read

her diary, but you never knew. She glanced at the clothbound book and ran her finger over the flimsy lock. A two-year-old could jimmy this thing open. Maybe she'd better keep her thoughts to herself. She didn't want to get her sister into hot water.

Tessa closed the diary and slipped it into the drawer of the bedside table. Leaning against the pillows, she thought back to last night. When she'd first seen Tammy holding that bottle, she was sure she was joking. But two seconds later Tammy had pulled out some paper cups from the other boot, whipped a corkscrew out of her purse, opened the wine bottle, and poured them both a drink.

Tessa hadn't had the nerve to tell her sister that she didn't want any. That was weird, too, she thought; normally, she didn't have a problem saying no. For goodness' sake, she'd made it all the way through high school without touching booze, and that had taken courage. But last night, her spine had turned into a noodle.

She'd taken the wine and they'd started talking. Really talking. About everything. Friends, current events, books, and movies. She'd actually impressed her sister with the depth of her knowledge of the L.A. movie colony, sharing with her some of the gossip she'd picked up by listening in on Lorna's telephone sessions with her friends. It had been great. For the first time since learning about her trip to Santa Barbara, she'd felt good.

Then they'd started talking about clothes. Tammy opened her closet and Tessa had gaped like a country bumpkin. Her sister's closet was stuffed with Italian silk blouses, beautifully tailored skirts and jackets, elegant shoes, and enough accessories to stock a boutique. ''Doreen says I need to dress well,'' Tammy had said with a shrug. ''But it's more for her benefit than mine. She's always trying to drag me off to her charity functions. It's a real pain. If you want to, you can borrow them whenever you like.''

Tessa smiled as she remembered this conversation. Her sister didn't shop at discount stores. Some of those numbers she'd seen in Tammy's closet were designer originals. Then her smile faded as she remembered something else.

While she'd managed to make that one cup of wine last all evening, Tammy had drained the whole bottle by the time they were tired enough to call it quits and get some sleep.

Tessa finished writing in her diary and read in her room for a while before she went downstairs. She stuck her head in the dining room and saw that the remains of last night's dinner were gone. She made her way into the kitchen and stopped at the door. A small, white-haired woman was loading dishes into the dishwasher.

''Uh, excuse me,'' Tessa said.

The woman looked up and her eyes widened in surprise. ''My goodness, you really do look like your sister.''

''Well, yes, we're identical twins.'' Tessa smiled and introduced herself. She advanced toward the woman with her hand outstretched.

"I'm Margery Perkins." She wiped her hand on her apron and shook Tessa's hand. "I'm pleased to meet you. Would you like some breakfast?"

"No thank you, but if you don't mind, I'd like to make myself a cup of tea."

"I'll get it for you," Margery replied. "You go have yourself a seat." She gestured at the dining nook. "Are you sure you aren't hungry?"

The thought of food made her stomach hurt. Even though she hadn't had much wine, she now felt slightly nauseous. "No thanks, I'm not hungry."

"You're like your sister, then." Margery picked up the teakettle and took it to the sink. "She never eats breakfast either."

Tessa made polite small talk while she waited for her tea to boil. "Thank you," she said, taking the mug from Mrs. Perkins. "I think I'll go see if I can find Tammy."

"I think she's out by the pool." Mrs. Perkins waved in the direction of the backyard.

Tessa nodded. She walked back through the house, marveling at how quiet the place was. Mrs. Perkins must be some housekeeper, she thought as she stared into the silent living room. There wasn't a thing out of place. Not a book or a magazine or even so much as a piece of lint on the carpet. The house was beginning to remind Tessa of a department-store showroom; all the proper pieces were in place, but it didn't look like anyone lived there.

She went through the double French doors and onto the red tiled patio. At the end of the patio was a large, oval-shaped swimming pool surrounded by more tile and a lush green lawn. In the center was a round, white, wrought-iron table with matching chairs and two plump pillowed loungers. Tammy, wearing a red bikini, was lying on one of them. She had on a pair of huge designer sunglasses that Tessa knew must have cost at least fifty bucks. "Good morning," she said brightly.

"Morning," Tammy mumbled. "What time did you get up?"

"Hours ago." Tessa pulled up a lounger next to her sister and sat down. "But as the house was so quiet, I just stayed in my room and read for a while."

Tammy yawned. "I woke up about half an hour ago."

Tessa took a sip of the tea. "Where is everyone?" She had no idea what she was supposed to do now. No one had bothered to tell her what would be expected of her this summer. Was she just supposed to sit around this silent house?

"Harold's at work." Tammy yawned again. "And Doreen's probably at a committee meeting. That's what she usually does."

Tessa nodded. "Uh, what are we going to do today?"

Tammy shrugged. "I don't know about you, but I'm not planning on doing anything except lying on this lounger."

"Oh." Darn. This was worse than she'd thought. She'd hoped that Tammy might want to show her around town. Maybe she could at least find a book-store or the library.

"I've got a headache," Tammy explained.

"Is there a library around here?" Tessa was not going to do nothing all day.

"Of course there's a library," Tammy snapped. "This isn't Los Angeles, but we're not completely out in the boonies."

"I didn't mean to imply anything," Tessa said hastily. "It's just . . ."

"Oh, don't mind me." Tammy waved her hand dismissively. "These headaches always make me crabby. I'm sorry; okay?"

"Okay."

"Look, you're bored, right?"

Tessa couldn't deny it. "Well . . ." she hedged, "at home there's always tons of things to do."

"Why don't you take my car and drive into Lansdale." Tammy grinned. "Like I said, it ain't L.A., but there's some neat shops and a couple of bookstores."

Surprised, Tessa stared at her. "You'd let me drive your car?" One of the biggest disappoint-ments she'd felt when her parents had told her about her summer in Lansdale was that she wouldn't be able to work and save for her own car. The transportation issue had been a bone of con-tention between Tessa and her folks ever since she'd gotten her license. She wanted a car of her own. They insisted she was too young, it was too big an expense, she'd drive off a cliff, it was too dangerous, and what was wrong with the family Buick?

"Of course I would, silly." Tammy giggled. "I'm not going to use it."

"Wow, that's really cool." Tessa jumped to her feet. "I'll just run upstairs and get my hat."

"Your hat?" Tammy repeated incredulously.

Tessa smiled self-consciously. "Yeah, I know it sounds lame, but Mom drilled it into me never to go out in the sun without a hat."

"Oh yes, that's right, I suppose with her being an actress, she'd be worried about how the sun wrinkles you."

"That," Tessa replied, "and the fact that she's paranoid I'm going to get skin cancer." She glanced pointedly at Tammy. "We're fair-skinned. I've listened to more lectures about the rising rate of skin cancer among young people than most kids have had hot dinners. And I mean that literally. Mom tends to harp on stuff she thinks is important."

"Okay, go get your hat. While you're upstairs, feel free to dip into my closet. I've got some really great outfits that would look fabulous on you." She laughed. "I know, because they look great on me."

"You mean it?" Tessa couldn't believe her luck. Not only was she going to drive her sister's car, but she was going to wear one of those fabulous outfits.

"I wouldn't offer if I didn't mean it. We're sisters, right?"

"Right. I'll be back in a jiffy."

Tessa took the stairs two at a time, ran into Tammy's room, and threw open her closet. As her hand brushed along the colorful clothes she realized that the only tough part was going to be deciding what to wear. Finally, she settled on a red cotton sundress with tiny spaghetti straps and a dropped waist. She also found a pair of matching sandals. The dress might be cotton, but Tessa could tell by the feel of the material that it hadn't come from a discount store or a swap meet. The sandals were real leather, too.

Tessa flew into her room, slipped on the elegant dress, and then pulled her oversize straw hat out of the closet. Tucking her long hair up and securing it with some bobby pins, she slipped the sandals on, popped the hat on her head, and grabbed her sunglasses. When she surveyed herself in the mirror, she was pleased with the results. She looked cool and sophisticated. What a blast!

She hurried back downstairs and out to the patio. Tammy glanced up at her and her mouth dropped open. "God, you look just like me in that outfit."

"Yeah, cool, isn't it?" Tessa giggled. "What time do I have to be back?"

Tammy took her sunglasses off and frowned. "No particular time. I'm not planning on going anywhere today."

Tessa thought that was a little strange. Everyone at her house told each other where they were going and when they'd be back. It was a rule, it was set in stone, it was one of the commandments. But what the heck, this household was different. Tessa was sure now that she was going to like it here. "Okay, uh, where are the car keys?"

"On the table in the front hall." Tammy popped her glasses back on and leaned back against the lounger. "The car's in the garage, it's the white one."

"I'll see you later." Eager to explore, Tessa hurried out to the front door. On her way she ran into Doreen coming down the stairs. Doreen paused on the bottom step, her eyes surveying Tessa from head to toe.

"Tammy told me it was okay to borrow some of her clothes," Tessa said quickly.

"And you look very nice in them," Doreen said calmly. She flicked a piece of nonexistent lint off the sleeve of her own elegant, cream-colored silk blouse. "I'm just on my way out to a committee meeting. What are you up to?"

Tessa was really embarrassed now and she wasn't sure why. "Tammy said I could take her car into town and look around. She's got a headache."

"She gets a lot of headaches. I think it must be eyestrain. I'm going to insist she go to an ophthalmologist soon." Doreen nodded and walked out into the foyer. "I take it you do know how to drive?"

"Yeah, I've had my license for almost two years." Tessa laughed. "Never had an accident yet."

Doreen didn't crack a smile. She just opened the

front door and turned to Tessa. "Good, then I'll see you this evening."

With that, she left. Tessa sighed in relief, waited till she heard a car start up in the driveway, and then grabbed the remaining set of keys out of the crystal dish on the table.

Dashing out to the garage, she skidded to a halt as she saw the sleek white BMW convertible. "Wow," she murmured. She walked to the vehicle, opened the door, and climbed in. The seats were white, too. White leather. The expensive kind.

Tessa took a deep breath, put the key in the ignition, and turned on the engine. It fired right up. Barely breathing, she eased out of the driveway and onto the street.

The ride into Lansdale was short. Within ten minutes, she was cruising into the center of town. Tessa slowed down as she drove down the main street. She passed a row of smart shops and a strip mall. Finally, she came to a triangular strip of green grass bordered on each side by an official-looking building. Pulling in, she saw it was a park. Across the street was the city hall and library.

For the next two hours she explored the town. Even though there wasn't really all that much to see, she enjoyed herself immensely. Especially as she was driving such a great car. Around noon, she realized the rumblings from her belly were hunger pangs, so she pulled into a Mexican fast-food joint.

She parked Tammy's car as far away from other vehicles as possible, popped her sunglasses in her purse, and walked across the asphalt to the entrance. She reached for the handle on the front door. Suddenly hands grabbed her around the waist, whirled her around, and before she could react, she was hauled up against a male chest and kissed.

Tessa struggled to pull away. Her hat flew off, her hair slipped out of its twist, and her purse landed on the ground with a thud. She balled her hand into a fist like her dad had taught her and landed her attacker a hard one in the neck.

The blow wasn't as powerful as she'd hoped, and she'd been aiming for her assailant's nose not his neck. But he leaped back and yelped in surprise. "Hey," he cried. "What gives, Tammy? What's gotten into you? And where did you get that funny wig?" He leaned forward and grabbed a strand of Tessa's hair, gave it a good pull, and then gaped in shock when it didn't budge.

"It's not a funny wig, you jerk," Tessa snapped. "It's my hair." She slapped at his hand. "And I'll thank you to keep your paws off it and off me."

"Tammy?"

"I'm not Tammy." Tessa glared at the boy. He was one of the cutest guys she'd ever seen, but that didn't give him the right to maul her.

"Oh, my God." He started backing away. "I'm really sorry. I thought you were someone else. Look, this is really embarrassing." His cheeks turned red. "Honestly, you look enough like her to be her twin."

"I *am* her twin," she announced calmly. God, he was adorable. Dark blond hair, one of those faces with really good bone structure, and a pair of haunting, deep-set hazel eyes.

"You're Tammy's sister?" he said, surprise etched on his face.

"That's right. Who are you?"

"I'm Alex."

He said it like it was supposed to mean something to her. Tessa just stared at him suspiciously.

"Tammy's boyfriend," he continued, when her expression didn't change. "Honestly. We've been going together for two years."

"Funny, she never mentioned you to me."

"She never told me about you either," he shot back. "Heck, I didn't even know she had a sister."

"Well, she does." Tessa clamped her mouth shut. She had no idea what her sister had told her friends about the situation, and here was this guy, claiming to be Tammy's boyfriend. But Tammy had obviously not bothered to tell him a darned thing. What was she supposed to do or say now? Lansdale was a small town. Short of her becoming a hermit, people were going to notice that she looked like Tammy Mercer. "I'm Tessa Prescott."

"Alex Birkett." He suddenly smiled. "Let me buy you a Coke or something. I mean, to make up for my grabbing you the way I did."

Tessa debated about whether or not it was okay. Then she decided she really didn't have much choice. If this kid was anything like her friends at home and she didn't give him some kind of an explanation, there would be all kinds of wild stories about her and Tammy floating all over town. "I

was just going to get something to eat." She nodded toward the restaurant.

"Me, too." He reached for the door and held it
open for her. "They do great tacos here," he commented as they stepped inside.

"That sounds good." She followed him over to
the line of people waiting in front of the cash register.

"What'll you have?" he asked. "Get whatever
you like, I just got paid and I figure the least I can
do is buy your lunch."

"You don't have to do that," she said emphat-
ically. She noticed the girl behind the register was
staring at her with open curiosity.

"It's no big deal." Alex stepped up to the
counter and looked at Tessa inquiringly.

"Uh, I'll just have a taco and a root beer," she
said. The cashier was openly gaping at her now.
Tessa didn't know whether she should say something or not.

Alex turned to place their order, noticed the girl
staring goggle-eyed at Tessa, and grinned. "Hi,
Janine, that's Tammy's sister. She's new in town."

Janine cracked her gum and nodded. "I wondered if she was wearing a wig or something. You
sure that's Tammy's sister? Or is this some kind
of joke?"

Tessa didn't know whether or not she was supposed to speak up. Alex looked like he was enjoying himself, Janine was still staring at her, and
Tessa felt like she was standing on a street corner
stark naked. Some of the others behind the counter,

kids mostly, who looked to be about her own age, were now staring at her as well.

"It's no joke," Alex insisted. "She's really Tammy's sister."

"Tammy doesn't have a sister," the kid manning the milkshake machine called.

"But look at that hair," Janine called back. "I saw Tammy last week and she sure couldn't have grown it that long since then."

"Maybe it's a wig?" The girl wrapping tacos added her two cents' worth. "You know, one of those real expensive kinds that looks like real hair."

"Nah, it doesn't look like a wig," Janine yelled.

"Take it from me," Alex said loudly, "it's real hair. I should know, I just tried to yank it off."

Tessa wished the floor would open up and swallow her. The whole restaurant was now staring at her. "Uh, Alex," she said, "shouldn't you order?"

"Why? You in a hurry?" he asked, turning to grin at her. But he must have noticed the blush covering her cheeks, because the grin quickly turned to a sympathetic smile. "Sorry, this is probably kinda embarrassing for you."

"A little."

He nodded. "Come on, Janine, give us a break here," he said firmly. "We're hungry."

"All right." Janine grinned. "What'll you have?"

"Three tacos and two root beers."

She called the order into the little microphone beside the register and handed Alex his ticket stub.

Tessa gratefully followed him to a table.

"This is getting awkward," she murmured as they sat down at one of the small booths. "I hadn't realized that Tammy hadn't told anyone I was coming."

"Not even me," Alex replied. "Look, I'm sorry about what happened up there, I mean with everyone staring at you and all. But this has been a real surprise for us. None of us had a clue you even existed."

Moments later their number was called over the loudspeaker and Alex went to get their food. He came back carrying a tray. "So, have you been living with your dad or something?" he asked.

"Or something," she mumbled. For the first time in her life she didn't want to admit she was adopted. Tessa concentrated on unwrapping her taco. What could she say? That she was such a loser her own mother had given her away and kept her sister? This was so weird. She felt a surge of guilt rip through her and knew it came from feeling disloyal to her parents. But darn it. They weren't the ones sitting here being stared at like she was some kind of freak and having to answer really lousy questions.

"Tammy told me that Harold Mercer isn't her biological father." Alex bit into his taco. "So I figured you'd been living with her real dad."

Tessa finally looked up. Maybe he saw the confusion in her eyes or maybe it was because of the blush she could feel spreading across her face for the second time in less than ten minutes, but all of a sudden his expression changed.

"Hey." He put his food down. "I didn't mean to bug you with so many questions."

"It's okay," she said softly. "I know you're curious." She glanced around the room. Several of the kids behind the counter were still staring at her. "Everyone is."

"Yeah," he said, his gaze following her glance, "it looks like it." He turned back to her. "Maybe we shouldn't have come in here."

Tessa shrugged. "I'm going to be here all summer, I can't exactly hide. I just didn't think it would be like this. I mean, it's weird to have everyone so curious about me."

"Guess you haven't been living with your dad, huh?"

"You guessed right," she admitted. "I was adopted when I was a baby. My mother kept Tammy and gave me away." There, she'd said the words out loud. She was surprised at how good it felt. Why the heck should she feel bad about the situation? She'd only been a month old when it happened.

Alex didn't say anything for a moment. He reached for his root beer. "Must make you feel funny."

"A bit."

"Yeah, I can see that. Anyway, where are you from?"

"Los Angeles."

"Ah, the big city." He grinned. "Lansdale probably looks pretty small to you."

"It's not that small," she replied. The tension had gone and she found herself relaxing. "But I'm not used to being stared at so much."

"Don't worry; now that they've seen you"—he jerked his chin toward the kids behind the counter—"they'll spread the word, and by next week you'll be old news. Have you ever met Tammy before?"

She shook her head. "I didn't even know that I had a sister until last week. No one bothered to mention that we were twins, either. I had the shock of my life when I got off that airplane yesterday."

"I'll bet." He smiled sympathetically. "And you really do look alike."

"If I cut my hair, could you tell us apart?" Tessa wondered why she'd asked such a dumb question, but Alex seemed to take it seriously. From across the table, he was studying her intently.

"I'm not sure," he finally admitted. "Maybe. But then again, maybe not. I'd have to see you together. Hey, why don't you come to the party with Tammy tonight."

"What party?" Tessa asked. Tammy hadn't mentioned that she was going out. But then, there were a number of things, one of which was sitting right across from her, that Tammy hadn't mentioned.

"A bunch of us are getting together at Jeremy's house. His folks are in San Francisco."

"I don't know," she said hesitantly. An unchaperoned party? Tessa knew her parents would have a fit if they knew. Not that she'd never been to an unchaperoned party before. But she'd had to do some fancy footwork to get away with it. Somehow, though, she had a strong feeling that Doreen and Harold wouldn't mind in the least. Still, Alex was Tammy's boyfriend. She didn't want to cause any trouble with her sister. "Maybe I ought to see if Tammy invites me."

"Tammy won't mind," he replied quickly. "Take my word for it, she won't care. Besides, it would be a good chance for you to meet everyone."

"I don't know. I don't want to be rude. I'm a houseguest, remember?" Tessa was really tempted. Alex seemed nice and it would be great to meet some new people. But she still wasn't sure. "Tammy didn't mention any plans for tonight."

"She probably just assumed you'd be going with her," he suggested eagerly. "Either that, or she forgot."

"Tammy wouldn't forget a date."

Alex laughed. To Tessa's ears it sounded a bit sarcastic, but then she decided she didn't know him well enough to make that kind of a judgment. "These days," he said cryptically, "Tammy forgets a lot of things. Look, I don't want to put you on the spot, so why don't I give you my phone number? When you get home, ask Tammy about tonight. If she's coming, come with her. If she's not coming, give me a call and I'll pick you up. You got a pen or something?"

Tessa dug in her purse for a pen. As she handed it across the table a nasty suspicion crossed her mind. "Hey, you guys aren't fighting or anything, are you?"

"Nah." He scribbled on a napkin and then handed it to Tessa. "We're not fighting."

"And you *are* her boyfriend, right?" Tessa was very puzzled.

"Sure. Only a complete idiot would lie about something you could check so easily." He leaned back against the booth and crossed his arms over his chest. "Any more questions?"

"Okay, if you must know. If you're going together," Tessa pressed, "and you're not fighting, then how come you say that Tammy might not want to go to the party tonight?"

Alex didn't answer for a minute. Finally, he said, "Let's just say that Tammy hasn't been too sociable lately, okay?"

No, Tessa thought, it wasn't okay. But from the tone of his voice and the set of his jaw, she didn't think it would do her any good to ask any more questions. Besides, why should she care about Tammy and Alex's relationship? It wasn't any of her business. The guy was just being nice. Going out of his way to make her feel welcome. But then why did she get the strangest feeling that there was something else going on, something that Alex wasn't telling her?

"You want to come, or not?" Alex asked.

Tessa gave up trying to figure things out. What the heck. How often did she get invited to a party? "I'd love to go," she replied.

CHAPTER THREE

June 20, Emergency Entry
Dear Diary,
I know I've already written in you today, but this is an emergency. Alex Birkett is about the cutest guy I've ever met and he's my sister's boyfriend. Not that that's the emergency or anything, but I felt I ought to be totally honest here. I'm not going to move in on Tammy either, I've always hated girls who move in on someone else's boyfriend. But it's kind of a shame I never met a guy like Alex down in L.A. Anyway, on to my problem. I DON'T HAVE ANY IDEA WHAT THE HECK I'M SUPPOSED TO TELL PEOPLE! After all those weird looks I got today in the taco joint, I realized that people are going to be curious. Oh, what the heck, people are just plain nosy. It's so embarrassing to tell people I was adopted. From the way Alex talked, everyone knows that Tammy wasn't.

I'm not ashamed of my parents or anything like that, but they don't know what it's like to walk into a room and have everyone stare at you like you've just grown another head. I might as well have a big sign saying LOSER written on my forehead.

Tessa read the words she'd just written and winced. She felt like a snake. No. Lower than a snake; she felt like a worm. Her parents would be devastated if they ever saw what she'd written. But she had to express her feelings somewhere. At least writing it in her diary was better than sharing it with them.

"Hey, Tessa, you in there?" Tammy called through the closed bedroom door.

"Come on in." Tessa tossed her diary back in the bedside table just as Tammy stepped inside.

"Hi," Tammy said. "I thought I heard you come back."

"It looked like you were asleep when I peeked in your room," Tessa explained. "I didn't want to wake you up."

"I wasn't really sleeping." Tammy flopped onto the foot of her bed and yawned. "Just dozing. That's all I've done all day, lie around. So, how do you like our little town?"

"It's not that little," Tessa said. She could smell a faint odor of peppermints. The scent seemed to be coming off her sister.

"Stop being polite," Tammy snorted in derision. "Compared to L.A., Lansdale is Podunk Junction, USA."

"I think it's neat," Tessa said. "You don't have traffic jams, smog, drive-by shootings, and crazies wandering the streets. I saw the library, the mall, and the park."

"Then you saw it all. I'm so bored with this place, I could scream. There's absolutely nothing to do around here."

"There was one of those multiplex movie theaters at the mall," Tessa said, wondering why she felt the urge to defend the place. "And I saw two video stores."

"Yeah, but there's more to life than movies."

"I ran into a friend of yours," Tessa said hesitantly.

Tammy perked up. "Who?"

"Alex. He says he's your boyfriend."

"He is my boyfriend," Tammy said firmly. "Where did you meet him?"

Tessa decided maybe she ought to omit a few of the details about her meeting with Alex today. Tammy might not like knowing that he had kissed her, thinking she was Tammy. "At the taco stand on Twin Oaks Boulevard. He thought I was you."

"I see." Tammy stared directly at her.

For some odd reason, Tessa felt guilty. The feeling, one which she'd had far too often in the last two days, was very annoying. "How come you didn't mention him last night?" she asked.

Tammy shrugged. "Why should I? You didn't give me a list of the guys you've dated."

"No, but I told you there wasn't anyone special. Alex told me the two of you have been going together for two years," Tessa said earnestly. "When we ran into each other today, he thought I was you. It was really embarrassing."

"But your hair's a good foot longer than mine," Tammy countered.

"I had my hat on," Tessa replied. "And he wasn't the only one staring at me either. Everyone who works at that taco joint was staring at me. I didn't know what to say."

Tammy's eyes narrowed in confusion. "Say about what? And what's that got to do with Alex?"

Tessa closed her eyes briefly. She wasn't making any sense. "Let me start at the beginning." Taking a deep breath, she told her sister what had happened at the restaurant, omitting only the fact that Alex had kissed her. "So you see," she finished, "I don't know what to say to people. It's really no one's business that I was adopted, but you know how nosy people are. They'll ask anyway."

Tammy thought about it for a moment and then shrugged. "Tell people whatever you like. I don't see what the problem is. Like you said, it's no one's business."

"Not even your boyfriend's?"

Tammy looked at her sharply. "Why do you say that?"

"Because he was sure asking a lot of questions."

"Alex is the curious type," Tammy admitted. "What did you tell him?"

"The truth." Tessa shrugged. "But it would

have been a lot easier on me if you'd said something to him earlier.''

"You mean, before you got here."

Tessa nodded. Now Tammy was getting it. If her sister had laid the groundwork a little better, she wouldn't have to be fending off these embarrassing questions. "Yeah. I mean, he *is* your boyfriend, right? So of course he'd be curious."

"I guess he would," Tammy agreed.

"You really should have told me about him."

"Just because we share a genetic bond doesn't mean we have to tell each other everything," Tammy replied casually.

"Yeah, I guess so." Tessa was hurt, but she struggled not to let it show. "There's plenty I haven't told you. Oh, Alex wanted me to remind you about the party tonight."

"I didn't forget," Tammy said defensively. "Honestly, sometimes Alex treats me like a two-year-old."

"So you're going?"

"Naturally. Anything's better than hanging around here. I was planning on asking you to tag along."

Tessa's pride was wounded by Tammy's choice of words. That was twice now in two minutes. She started to tell her sister that she would rather stay home, but then decided that cutting off her nose to spite her face was dumb. Maybe Tammy wasn't the most tactful person in the world. She probably didn't realize how hurtful she sounded. Besides, staying home alone with Doreen and Harold sounded about as much fun as a visit to the dentist. "I don't know, I'd hate to be a third wheel." Pride demanded that she not give in too quickly.

"Don't be so sensitive. There'll be a lot of people there without dates."

"Is Alex picking you up?"

"No, he's working till almost eight tonight. He's got a part-time job at a video store. I'll meet him there."

"What kind of clothes are you wearing?" Tessa hoped the casual outfits she'd brought along would be okay.

"Whatever. If you don't like the clothes you brought from home, you're welcome to raid my closet." Tammy got up off the bed. "I'm going to get something to eat. You hungry?"

"No, not really. I think I'll go for a walk. I could use the exercise."

Tammy paused at the door. "Oh, your mom called while you were out. And there's a letter from Mexico for you in the hall downstairs. What did they do, write it before they left?"

Tessa laughed. "Probably. Did Mom say she'd call back?"

"She said they were going out on location to shoot and she'd check in with you tomorrow morning around seven." Tammy looked at her curiously. "They keep pretty close tabs on you, don't they?"

"Yeah, I guess so."

"Any reason?"

Confused, Tessa stared at her sister. "I'm their

kid; of course they want to know what's going on with me. Why?''

"Oh, I don't know, I just wondered if maybe you'd gotten in bad trouble or something and they were checking up on you.''

Tessa shook her head. ''I've never gotten in any real trouble. They just like to know that I'm all right, that's all.''

"Okay. Be ready to roll around seven-thirty.'' Tammy started to close the door.

"What about dinner?'' Tessa asked. ''What time do we eat?''

"Whenever you get hungry. There's loads of stuff in the freezer.'' She burped slightly and quickly covered her mouth with her hand. But that didn't stop Tessa from getting a whiff of what was on Tammy's breath. Even from across the room she could identify the smell. It was wine.

"Today's Friday,'' her sister continued. ''That means Harold will go straight to the country club after work and Doreen will probably join him there for dinner.''

Tammy wasn't ready to go until almost seven forty-five. Tessa waited impatiently in the foyer, occasionally glancing at herself in the gilt-edge decorator mirror over the table and fretting over her choice of clothes. The tailored brown slacks and cream-colored silk blouse outlined her slim figure perfectly, but she wasn't sure it was the right thing to wear to a party. Maybe the kids around here dressed funkier or more casually. Maybe she ought to run upstairs and throw on a pair of jeans.

Tammy's voice cut into her thoughts. "Sorry it took me so long. But I couldn't decide what to wear."

Tessa turned and surveyed her sister curiously. Tammy was dressed in a red skirt slit halfway to her thigh and a matching silk tank top. Ruefully, she glanced down at her own outfit and felt like a frump. Apparently the kids around here dressed up for parties.

Tammy paused by the bottom step and pulled her car keys out of the tiny red purse swinging by her side. "Do you want to drive?"

"Sure," Tessa cried excitedly. "That's really nice of you," she began.

"It's no biggie." Tammy shrugged, tossed her the keys, and headed for the front door. "I know you don't have a car."

Grinning from ear to ear, Tessa followed her sister out to the garage. They got into the car, buckled their seat belts, and then Tessa turned the ignition on.

Tammy leaned toward the steering wheel, her gaze narrowing as she studied the fuel indicator. "How much gas is left?"

"Plenty. I filled it up when I was out." Tessa wrinkled her nose as she caught another whiff of Tammy's breath. She glanced at her sister. Maybe Tammy wasn't letting her drive because she was nice; maybe she was letting her play chauffeur because she herself didn't dare risk getting behind the wheel. Although Tammy had sprayed herself with

perfume and used plenty of peppermint mouthwash, Tessa's sharp senses had caught a faint, familiar odor. Wine again. Tammy must have been
drinking this afternoon. What was with this girl?

"You don't have to do that," Tammy said, set-
tling back in her seat. "Harold can afford to keep
this car gassed. Next time, unless you're running
on fumes, bring it home."

"Okay." Tessa nodded. She wondered if she
should ask Tammy about the booze and then decided she didn't want to stick her nose in her sister's business. After all, Tammy had made it quite
clear that just because they shared a genetic bond,
that didn't mean they bared their souls to each
other.

"This party ought to be a blast," Tammy said
as Tessa slowly pulled the car out of the driveway.
"Hey, you don't have to drive like an old lady,
I've got good insurance."

"Sorry," Tessa murmured. "Where to?"

"Go straight down the street and turn left."
Tammy pointed down the hill. "It's only a few
minutes from here. We could have walked, but
heck, that's a drag. Anyway, like I was saying, we
ought to have a good time if everyone doesn't blow
it big time by making too much noise."

Tessa reached the bottom of the hill and turned.
"Where to now?"

"Keep going straight. Jeremy's place is two
streets over. It's the big house on the corner. Once
you get past Markham Place, go ahead and park."

Despite Tammy's comment, Tessa drove carefully, concentrating on getting the expensive car to their destination in one piece.

"I sure hope Jeremy still has that police scanner," Tammy muttered as they got out of the car.

"Police scanner?" Tessa closed her door and made sure it was locked.

"Yeah, it'll come in handy if one of his nosy neighbors calls the cops. We can at least get a few minutes' warning." Tammy grinned at her. "Neat, huh? Feel free to imbibe freely. We can always walk home if the cops come."

Amazed, Tessa followed her sister down the block and up a brick walkway into a house that was just as large as the Mercers'. Geez, were all of Tammy's friends rich?

Tessa took a long, deep breath and rubbed her palms on her thighs as Tammy rang the doorbell. Heck, she still hadn't decided what to tell people if they started asking her questions.

A tall, gangly boy with bright red hair and ten million freckles stuck his head out the front door. Like the kids working at the fast-food restaurant, his eyes widened when he saw the two girls standing in front of him. "Geez! Bobby Talmadge wasn't joking. You two really do look alike. I didn't believe it when he called me." He grinned at Tessa. "You've been a well-kept secret," he said.

"Is Alex here yet?" Tammy pushed past the kid into the house.

Feeling awkward, Tessa smiled nervously.

Tammy could have at least introduced her. "Hi, I'm Tessa Prescott."

"I'm Jeremy Fiske. Come on in, everyone wants to meet you."

By the time they walked down the long hall and into what Tessa assumed was the family room, she'd completely lost sight of her sister.

"Hey everyone," Jeremy yelled to the crowded room. "This is Tammy's twin, Tessa."

Everyone in the room turned and stared. Tessa felt like she was standing naked in the middle of the mall. She didn't know whether to wave, smile, or start doing jumping jacks. So she just stood next to Jeremy smiling idiotically and wanting to kill her sister. Why had Tammy dumped her in a roomful of strangers and disappeared? There were at least twenty people gaping at her. "Uh, hi," she mumbled.

"Hi, Tessa." Alex stepped out of a group that was clustered near the corner and waved. "Over here."

Gratefully, she fled in his direction. "Hi. I thought you didn't get off work till later," she said quickly.

"My boss came in early and took pity on me. I'm glad you could make it," he said, giving her a friendly grin. There were three other kids standing in a semicircle around him. "This is Tom Hallard." Alex nodded toward a pale-faced boy with dark brown hair and the beginnings of a goatee on his chin. "And this is Joleen Lykstra." He indicated a petite blonde standing beside Tom. "This is Pete Barker.'' He introduced the last of the group, a short boy with the curliest black hair Tessa had ever seen.

Joleen stared at her in amazement. ''Man, except for the hair, you look just like Tammy.''

''Well, uh, we *are* twins.'' Tessa felt a flash of resentment. Even though she could hear people talking in the background, she was aware that half the people in the room were still staring at her. She was getting tired of the feeling.

''Have you been living with your dad?'' Joleen pressed.

''No, uh . . .''

''Geez, Joleen,'' Alex interjected. ''Give it a rest. The poor girl hasn't even had time to get something to drink and you're nailing her with questions.''

''I'm just curious,'' Joleen said defensively. ''It's not like Tammy ever said anything about her.''

Alex took Tessa's arm and led her toward the other side of the room. ''Come on. Let's get something to drink.''

''Thanks,'' Tessa murmured as they pushed their way through the crowd. ''That was getting awkward. I'm not exactly sure how to answer people yet when they ask me those kinds of questions.'' Again, she felt a surge of resentment, only this time it was directed at Doreen Mercer—she couldn't bring herself to think of the woman as ''Mother''. One part of her felt like she'd been dumped on the auction block and sold at half price. ''It's kinda hard to tell Tammy's friends I was adopted. I mean, most people probably know that she wasn't—'' She broke off as she realized how lame she sounded.

But Alex didn't seem to notice. ''Don't let it bother you,'' he said sympathetically as they came to a table loaded with beer and soft drinks. ''What do you want?''

''I'll have a Coke,'' she replied, hoping that didn't sound too childish to Alex. Then she was mad at herself for caring what he thought. For goodness' sake, he was Tammy's boyfriend.

Alex studied her a moment, his expression curiously bland. ''You don't like beer?''

Tessa wasn't going to wake up tomorrow feeling nauseous, not even to impress a boy. ''Not much.''

''So you don't drink?'' he pressed

''No,'' she said defensively. ''I don't. It makes me half-sick.''

''Yeah.'' He grinned suddenly. ''It makes me want to throw up, too.'' He reached for a couple of cans of Coke. ''These okay?''

At that moment Tammy appeared out of the crowd and draped her arm around Alex's waist. ''Hi, you two,'' she said pleasantly. ''This is some party, isn't it?'' She glanced at Alex. ''I've been looking everywhere for you.''

''I've been right here for the past half hour,'' he replied.

''You having a good time?'' Tammy asked Tessa.

As they'd only been there five minutes, Tessa

thought it was too early to tell one way or another, but she didn't want to be rude. "It's been interesting," she commented.

Tammy let go of Alex and leaned across him to pick up a can of beer.

"I hope we can do a little better than 'interesting,' " Joleen put in, coming up and grabbing Alex around the waist.

Tessa glanced at her sister, wondering if Tammy would get mad at seeing Joleen's embracing Alex. But Tammy didn't look like she minded in the least. She had a glassy-eyed smile on her face.

"How come we never met you before?" Tom asked Tessa as he and Pete joined the group.

"Because it's her first time in Lansdale," Tammy answered for her sister.

"Where are you from?" Pete asked her.

Now that Tom had started the ball rolling, Tessa guessed it was open season. She opened her mouth to reply, but before she could get the words out, Tammy answered for her again.

"She lives in L.A. In the Hollywood Hills."

"Is that where your dad lives?" Joleen asked.

"No," Tessa replied quickly. She was getting a little irritated with Tammy for being her mouthpiece. Besides, on this question she wanted to do the talking. She'd die before she'd admit to a roomful of strangers that she had no idea who her father was. "I live with my parents. I was adopted."

"Adopted?" Joleen repeated the word as if she'd never heard it before.

"Yeah, dummy." Pete made a face at the petite

blonde. "Don't you know what it means?"

"Of course I know what it means," she snapped. "But Tammy isn't adopted, are you?"

Tammy ignored the question. "Tessa's parents are in the movie business," she said smoothly. "Her mother's an actress and her father's a director."

Whether it was intended to divert the flow of conversation or not, it worked, because Tessa was immediately inundated with questions about movie stars. Pete and Tom wanted to know if she'd ever met Sylvester Stallone. Joleen and another girl wanted to know if she'd ever seen Brad Pitt. When she told them she had, they demanded to know whether or not he was as good-looking in person as he was onscreen.

By the time Tessa got through fending off questions, she was surprised to notice that her sister was nowhere to be seen.

"Excuse me," Tessa said to a thin, brown-haired girl with glasses whose name she hadn't heard. "But I'd better go see if I can find Tammy."

She scanned the group in the family room and then pushed into the kitchen. No Tammy. Tessa had started for the double French doors that led to the patio when she felt someone grab her arm.

"Hey, where are you off to?" Alex asked.

"I wondered where Tammy is. I thought maybe she'd gone outside."

"Is something wrong?" Alex's expression turned serious. "I mean, have the kids been bugging you with a lot of questions?"

"No." She smiled at his consideration. "I just thought I'd see what my sister was up to."

"I see." He gazed at her thoughtfully and then jerked his chin toward the other side of the house. "Tammy's down there in one of the back bedrooms."

Tessa looked and saw nothing but a long, dark hall. "What's she doing?" She asked before she could stop herself. After all, she wasn't her sister's chaperon.

"Drinking," Alex answered shortly. "And I don't mean just beer either. Some of the kids get into some real hard stuff at parties like this. Tammy's with them."

Tessa started for the hall. "Maybe I should make sure she's all right," she began, but Alex's words stopped her.

"She won't thank you for it."

Tessa whirled around and looked at him. Again, he was watching her with a weird, kind of suspicious expression. Maybe he thought she was interfering too much in her sister's life. But what business was it of his? Then she realized that he'd known Tammy longer than she had. Besides, she thought, he'd probably been in there boozing with Tammy, too. Maybe she should back off. "Okay," she replied uneasily.

"You want to go outside and get some air?" he asked.

Coming from anyone else, she would have thought this was a line. But as Alex was her sister's boyfriend, she decided he meant exactly what he said. "It's pretty hot in here."

They went through the French doors and out onto the patio. The night air was refreshingly sweet after the confines of the room. When Alex wandered over toward a redwood picnic table and plopped down on the bench, Tessa decided to join him.

"It's really nice up here," she said conversationally. "Kinda different from L.A."

"Yeah, I guess it's quieter. Probably more quiet than you're used to."

She laughed. "Not really. I lead a pretty tame life. I only mean that it's less crowded, less frantic up here."

"So what do you do for entertainment when you're home?" he asked. He sounded as though he were genuinely interested, not just making conversation.

"Well, don't tell anyone, but my favorite thing to do is read."

"Yeah?" He grinned broadly. "Your secret's safe with me. I love to read, too. What kinda stuff?"

"Everything," Tessa replied. "Horror, romance, spy thrillers, sci-fi. Once I was so desperate, I read a treatise on Black Angus cattle."

Alex laughed. Before long, they were talking like they'd known each other all their lives. From books, they moved on to movies, school, parents, and a dozen other things. They would probably have continued talking for hours except that Jeremy stuck his head out and interrupted them. "Hey, you guys," he yelled. "You'd better make tracks. Danny just heard on the scanner that the cops are on their way."

"Hell," Alex cursed. "It's probably old Mrs. Carberry. She hates it when Jeremy has a party." He got up and started toward the house.

"But why?" Tessa asked. "We haven't been loud."

"She hates Jeremy," Alex replied. "You'd better round up Tammy and head home."

But Tammy was already in the foyer of the house, leaning against the banister and grinning woozily. "Hi, you guys." She hiccuped softly.

"Damn," Alex muttered softly. "She's already plastered."

"I'll drive home," Tessa said.

"I'd better help you get her to the car." Alex put his arm around Tammy. She giggled and snuggled close against him. Tessa fumbled in her pocket and located the car keys.

"Can you walk?" Alex asked Tammy.

"No, but I can fly." Tammy laughed again. She pulled away from Alex and stumbled toward the front door, flapping her arms.

As everyone else was leaving, there was quite a crowd pouring out of the family room, and they hooted with laughter at Tammy.

"Geez, Tammy." Alex grabbed her and pulled her none too gently through the front door. "You're making an ass of yourself."

"Hey, you don't have to be so rough with her," Tessa cried as she ran after them.

But Alex didn't stop, he just pulled a giggling Tammy behind him. "Where's the car?" he snapped, glancing over his shoulder at Tessa.

She pointed down the block. "Over there."

"Good. Run on ahead and get the passenger-side door open." He gave Tammy, who had stumbled slightly, a hard tug. "Come on, Tam."

Tessa couldn't stand his roughness anymore. "Knock if off," she yelled. "Don't pull at her like that! She's going to fall and hurt herself if you keep yanking her around."

By this time they had reached the car. Alex glared at Tessa, grabbed the keys from her hand, and unlocked the door. Shoving Tammy inside, he jerked her seat belt across her chest and locked it into place. Then he slammed the door so hard that Tessa jumped three feet. "You don't get it, do you? The cops are on the way and she's drunk. You've got to get out of here."

"But you didn't have to be so hard on her," Tessa protested weakly. "She's not the first kid to get drunk. Everyone does it occasionally."

The car was parked under a streetlight, so Tessa could see Alex's face quite clearly. It was clear to her that his smile was bitter and his expression hard.

"Occasionally is the key word," he said. "With your sister, it's a bit more than that."

"Okay, even if it is, she's not the only one who

was drinking tonight.'' Tessa felt she ought to defend Tammy.

But Alex was quickly losing patience. He made a quick, chopping gesture with his hands and looked anxiously down the street. ''Let's not argue about this now. The cops are going to be here any minute. Even with the scanner, the station's not too far away. Go on, get moving. I don't want to be here when they arrive either. My parents are actually beginning to think I might be turning into a responsible adult. The last thing I need is to get busted at a drunken party.'' He walked around and opened the car door for Tessa. ''Get going. I'll follow you home to make sure you get there all right.''

Tessa jumped in behind the wheel and closed the door. Driving cautiously, she was turning onto the street where the Mercers lived when a police car passed her. She shivered. A close call. She had a feeling that Doreen and Harold wouldn't have liked it if their evening at the country club had been ruined by a call from the Lansdale Police Department.

CHAPTER FOUR

Dear Diary,
There's only one word to describe what my life
has been like the past couple of weeks: amazing.
I can't believe how little Doreen and Harold are
home. Even yesterday, the Fourth of July, they
went to dinner and a fireworks display at the
country club. But get this, they didn't invite
Tammy and me. As they were leaving, Doreen
muttered something about it being a boring,
"grown-up" function. I guess that was her way
of explaining why we hadn't been invited. But
since when have fireworks been for adults? I know
that with my parents there's too much together-
ness, but honestly, with these people, it's like
they're ships passing in the night. All the Mercers
ever do is hand out spending money and tell us
to have a good time. Not that I object to that. The

truth is, I have been having a pretty good time.
Tammy and I are getting closer, I've gotten to
know all her friends, and I've spent a lot of time
with Alex.

Tessa stared at the words she'd just written and bit
her lip. Alex was her sister's boyfriend, she had to
remember that. So what if he treated Tammy more
like a buddy than a girlfriend, that didn't mean he
didn't care for her.

Tessa wouldn't interfere in their relationship; no
matter how tempted she was to do so, she wouldn't
come between them. But darn, she thought with a
frown, what was she supposed to do?

Alex hung around all the time. It was getting
really tough to ignore the feelings that she had
started to have for him. In the past couple of weeks
she and Alex had gotten close. Real close. They
had so much in common. They liked the same
movies, the same books, the same TV shows. There
was always something to talk about. That wouldn't
normally be a problem for Tessa. She was buddies
with lots of guys back home, only they didn't send
her pulse racing and her heartbeat soaring every
time they walked into the room. Alex did.

It wouldn't be so bad if Tammy were around,
she thought dismally. Only the problem was, half
the time Tammy was nowhere to be seen. She generally spent her afternoons upstairs in her room,
supposedly taking a nap or nursing a headache.

Tessa snorted derisively. Sleeping, my foot, she
thought. Tammy was either up there chugging back

the booze or nursing a hangover. The few times she had stirred herself to come downstairs during one of Alex's visits, she'd parked herself on a lounger and been about as talkative as a dummy. Tessa sighed and shut her diary. She hoped Tammy wouldn't pull one of her "I have a headache" numbers tonight. It was Alex's birthday and they were supposed to be taking him out to dinner to celebrate.

Tessa wondered why Doreen and Harold didn't notice how fast their wine supply disappeared. But then again, she thought, considering that they had the stuff delivered by the case, an awful lot of it would have to be gone before they'd catch on to the fact that their daughter was helping herself liberally. Besides, Tammy was pretty careful. Tessa had seen her sister sneaking down to the pantry after a delivery. She never took more than a couple of bottles and only then from the back of the shelves.

A soft knock on her door interrupted her thoughts. Thinking it was Tammy, Tessa yelled, "It's open, come on in," then started in surprise when Doreen stepped inside and quietly shut the door behind her.

"Hi," Doreen said. "Are you busy?"

"Not at all," Tessa replied. Doreen looked different. It took her a moment to realize that underneath her perfect makeup, she was quite pale.

"Good, then I'd like to talk to you, if you don't mind." Doreen cleared her throat and glanced at the stool in front of the dressing table. "May I sit down?"

"Sure." Tessa stared at her curiously as she crossed the bedroom. Doreen's normally smooth walk was hesitant, almost jerky, her shoulders were ramrod straight, and as she sat down in front of the dressing table, she curled and uncurled her hands into fists.

"What's up?" Tessa asked curiously.

Doreen dropped her gaze and plucked at some nonexistent lint on her skirt. "Well," she began, "you've been here over two weeks now and you seem to have settled in quite nicely."

Tessa wasn't sure she liked the sound of that. "It's been fun. I've enjoyed myself."

"I thought we'd better have a talk."

"About what?" Tessa asked suspiciously. Was she in for a lecture? Maybe Tammy staying in her room most afternoons wasn't normal. Maybe Doreen was going to tell her to pack her bags.

Doreen hesitated. "This is rather difficult," she began, and Tessa's heart sank. "You see, I realize you're probably curious about some things."

Tessa was momentarily relieved. They weren't going to get rid of her. Then the meaning of Doreen's words sank in. She was on the verge of swearing that she wasn't curious about anything and really, why don't they just let the past stay dead and buried, when Doreen went on to say, "Things you have a right to be curious about." Her tone was determinedly bright. "Things you have a right to know."

But Tessa didn't want to know.

She didn't want to hear. There was only one topic that Doreen could possibly want to talk about. Tessa wished with all her heart that a 6.8 earthquake would hit at this very minute, preferably with the epicenter right under the Mercers' living room. "Uh, look," she began quickly. "I'm not all that—"

But Doreen didn't seem to hear her; her eyes had taken on a glazed look. It was like she was no longer there in the room, but was staring backward, into the past. "I was broke and pregnant," she blurted out.

Tessa stared at her.

"But I was going to keep my baby," Doreen continued. "My parents kicked me out when they found out. But I had a job. I was going to keep the baby." She paused. "Then I had two babies."

A cold hand clutched at Tessa's heart. She didn't want to hear any more of this. She couldn't. "Twins. You had twins."

Doreen nodded. "Yes. The delivery wasn't easy. I was in pretty bad shape. And then one of them was sick, so sick. They wouldn't let me take it from the hospital. They said if I did, it would die."

Tessa wanted to scream at her. This was a child, not an "it." But she couldn't get her voice to work. She couldn't get the words out.

"I couldn't take care of two of them," Doreen murmured. She clenched her hands together in her lap. "I couldn't take care of both of them. I had no money. One of them was sick. I couldn't do it."

"So you gave me away," Tessa finished. Once the words were said aloud, she found that the pain was gone. In its place was a great flat slab of nothingness, which made her feel numb.

"I didn't have enough money," Doreen said, then suddenly looked at Tessa. "And you were so sick. You cried all the time. All the time. The other one didn't."

One of them was sick.... You cried all the time.... The words echoed in Tessa's brain. Second best. Damaged goods. Her mother had given her away because she wasn't as good as her sister.

At that moment there was a pounding on the closed bedroom door and Tessa heard Tammy's voice calling, "Mom." Tammy stepped inside without waiting for an answer. "You've got a phone call," she said to her mother. "It's Mrs. Craddock."

"Tell her I'll call her back."

"But she says it's urgent," Tammy insisted. "She's practically hysterical. Something about the crab cakes for the summer ball."

"I'd better go and talk to her. She's utterly useless when it comes to handling caterers." Doreen stood up and smiled weakly at Tessa. "I'll talk to you later, dear." With that, she hurried toward the door. Tammy leaped out of her way as she rushed past.

Stunned and unable to move, Tessa stared at the departing form of the woman who'd given her life.

"What was that all about?" Tammy asked. She

plopped down on Tessa's bed. "Doreen having one of her heart-to-hearts with you?"

"She wanted to tell me why she'd given me away," Tessa muttered.

"Yeah," Tammy snorted. "Well, don't make a federal case out of it. From the way I see it, you were the lucky one."

Tessa ignored this remark. She knew that most kids had negative feelings about their parents. Besides, Tammy hadn't been the one given away. She wasn't the one who'd looked at herself in the mirror, trying to see what was so wrong with her that her own mother had unloaded her on complete strangers. Tessa cringed when she realized what she was thinking. She hadn't really indulged herself in ideas like that since she was fourteen. She knew that nothing was wrong with her. And nothing ever had been wrong with her, really. But there was one thing she wanted to know. One thing that had been bugging her ever since she'd found out the identity of her mother. "Tammy," she asked, "do you know who our father was?"

Tammy shrugged. "No one special. I asked Doreen about it once. She said it was some guy she was dating. He skipped town when she told him she was knocked up. Look, don't let Doreen and her little talks get to you. She only does it once in a blue moon. Usually after she's stumbled across some article in a women's magazine about openly communicating with your teenager. But these supermom phases don't last long."

"She gave me away because I cried all the

time,'' Tessa muttered. One part of her still couldn't believe what her birth mother had told her.

"Like I said, consider yourself lucky. At least you've got parents that care about you on a full-time basis, not just when they get a fast case of the guilts.''

Tessa studied herself in the foyer mirror as she waited for Tammy. Her sister had insisted that Tessa borrow something "special" for tonight. The aqua silk blouse and the contrasting multicolored palazzo pants were perfect. Tessa didn't understand why her sister, with a closetful of fabulous clothes, wanted to spend all her time shut up in her room. If she had a wardrobe like Tammy's, she'd be out every day, just to give herself an excuse to wear her gorgeous clothes.

"Come on, Tammy," she called. "It's almost eight o'clock.''

She turned as she heard footsteps on the stairs. Tammy, dressed in a pair of old jeans and an ugly gray sweatshirt, smiled wanly at her. "You're not going to believe this, but I've got one of my headaches. . . .'' she began.

"Take an aspirin.'' Tessa didn't want to be alone with Alex tonight. Instinctively, she knew it was wrong. Tammy should be with him on this of all nights. It was his eighteenth birthday.

"You know those don't work on my migraines,'' Tammy whined.

"But this is a special occasion,'' Tessa shot back. "Alex will be hurt if you don't come. You're his girlfriend and this is his eighteenth birthday.''

"Big deal. He'll have you to celebrate with."
Tammy started back up the stairs. "My head's
pounding like a jackhammer. I wouldn't be good
company tonight."

"But, Tammy," Tessa yelled. "What do I tell
him?"

"The truth. He'll understand. Alex knows I have
migraines. My car keys are on the table. Have a
good time."

Tessa shook her head. She felt bad for Alex—
he'd been expecting both girls to show up. She
quickly stifled the shaft of guilt that speared
through her, grabbed Tammy's car keys, and
headed for the front door. She refused to feel guilty
because Tammy wouldn't go out and celebrate
Alex's big night. It wasn't her fault, darn it.

Alex was waiting in front of the elegant steak
house when Tessa pulled into the parking lot. She
quickly found a space, parked, and hurried across
the asphalt. "Hi," she said cheerfully. "Happy
birthday."

He was wearing a tan sport coat, snazzy tie, and
pale blue shirt. He looked gorgeous. But he didn't
look happy. "Hi. Where's Tammy?"

"Uh, she had a headache," Tessa sputtered.

Alex's expression hardened.

"It's one of her bad ones, Alex," Tessa said
quickly. "A migraine."

"Yeah?" His mouth twisted cynically. "A migraine, huh."

"She said you'd understand," Tessa said softly.

She didn't know what to say to him. She really wished Tammy had come.

"That's me," he said brightly. "Mr. Understanding. Oh well, I guess it would be too much to expect her to drag her butt out on my account."

Disappointment washed over her like someone had just tossed a bucket of cold water on her head. Apparently, the idea of having dinner alone with plain old Tessa was too awful to contemplate. "Look," she said defensively, "Tammy didn't mean to get sick—"

"Sick," he repeated incredulously. "You really think she's got a headache?"

"Of course she does." Guilt nagged at her like a sore tooth. As much as she hated to admit it, one part of her had been secretly pleased at her sister's change of plans because it meant she would have Alex all to herself tonight. "If you'd like to call this off," she said quickly, "I'll understand."

Alex studied her for a moment, his expression stark. "Nah, we're here. We might as well celebrate. It's not every day you turn eighteen. Come on." He turned, yanked open the door, and stalked inside the restaurant.

Tessa had the feeling that continuing the evening as planned might not be a good idea, but in his present mood, she didn't want to argue with him. She followed him and stood silently next to him while he gave the hostess their names. A few moments later they were led to a booth.

Tessa slid in and tucked her small purse to one side. When she glanced up, Alex was looking at her, his expression openly speculative. "What's up?" she asked. "You're staring at me like I've got spots on my face."

"Sorry." He gave her a quick smile and then turned to the waiter, who was asking what they'd like to drink. They ordered soft drinks.

Twice, Tessa opened her mouth to talk, but both times, she backed off. Alex was obviously distracted, looking everywhere but at her. She glanced around the restaurant. It was a nice place. Elegant. White tablecloths and napkins, good heavy silverware, thick carpeting, and plenty of oak paneling, but the decor wasn't so fabulous that you needed ten minutes to take it all in.

Alex didn't speak until the busboy had brought them their Cokes. "You look really nice in that outfit."

Tessa smiled gratefully. Maybe he was over his snit. Maybe this evening wouldn't be a total wash. "Thank you."

"Tammy's?"

She nodded and her smile faltered at the tinge of sarcasm she caught in his tone. "She doesn't mind if I borrow her clothes."

"Or her car," he said. He picked up the menu and flipped it open. Tessa did the same. They both kept their heads hidden behind the open menus until the waiter came back and took their orders.

"How much longer are you staying?" Alex asked as soon as the man disappeared toward the kitchen.

Tessa jerked her head up. Again, she'd caught a

tinge of disapproval in his voice. "Just until September. Why?"

He shrugged. "No reason. I was just curious."

Tessa picked up her soft drink and took a sip. She wasn't thirsty, but it gave her a moment to think. Something was going on with Alex. He was upset and angry and trying hard not to let it show. She didn't think it was just because Tammy had bailed out, either. She'd gotten to know him in the past couple of weeks. Something else was going on. "You sounded more than just curious," she said softly. "What's up, Alex? I can see something's got you really bugged. What is it? The fact that Tammy's not here and I am?"

He drummed his fingers lightly against the tall glass in front of him. "It's not that," he admitted. "I didn't expect her to come. I mean, I'm getting used to her flaking out at the last minute. Especially when we'd planned to go somewhere where they check ID before bringing you a glass of wine."

"You're not being fair," Tessa protested. She felt she had to defend her sister. But one part of her wondered if she was really defending Tammy or merely justifying her own desire to spend more time alone with Alex. "She really does have a headache. You should have seen her. Her eyes were all sunken in and she was white as a sheet."

"Yeah, right." He didn't sound like he believed a word she said.

"Anyway, what does Tammy have to do with how long I'm staying in Lansdale?" Tessa asked.

He looked down at the table for a moment before

answering. "Don't take this the wrong way, but ever since you came, Tammy's gotten worse."

Stunned and speechless, Tessa stared at him. What was he talking about? Worse how? Good grief, he made it sound like Tammy had some major illness or something. Finally, she managed to ask, "What do you mean?"

Even in the dim light, she could see his cheeks flush with embarrassment. "Uh, forget I said anything," he began, but she cut him off.

"I won't forget it. This is my sister we're talking about. Do you know something I don't? And how have I made 'it'—whatever 'it' is—worse?"

Alex sighed. "Look, I didn't mean for it to sound like that. It's not like it's your fault or anything."

"What's not my fault?" Tessa was genuinely confused now. Hurt, too.

"Tammy. Her drinking. Ever since you came, she's gotten worse." He stopped talking as the waiter brought their dinners. Tessa glanced at her pepper steak and wondered if she could choke any of it down.

"I shouldn't have said anything," Alex said as soon as the waiter left them alone. "Just forget it, okay?"

She wanted to forget Alex's shocking observation, she really did. But after her little chat with Doreen today, after feeling once again like she'd had a label that read WORTHLESS slapped on her forehead at birth, she wasn't in any mood to placate

Alex. If she was hurting her sister, she wanted to know how and why.

"I can't do that," she said firmly. "I want to know exactly what you meant. How is my being here doing anything? I thought Tammy liked me. I thought we were getting along just fine."

"You are," he admitted honestly. "That's the problem." He jerked his head at her. "Just look at what you're wearing. It's Tammy's right?"

"Tammy insisted I go through her closet and pick something out," Tessa said defensively. "She was just being nice. Her clothes are a lot nicer than mine."

"Yeah, and by letting you wear her clothes and drive her car, she gets off free. Now she can sit up in her room and guzzle booze without even feeling guilty for ignoring her own sister."

"For crying out loud," Tessa snapped. "We've spent the past few weeks together, that's hardly 'ignoring' me. She's been great to me."

"Sure she has," he shot back. "You've been having such a good time this summer. You've been driving her wheels, wearing her clothes, and hanging out with her friends."

"What's wrong with that?"

"Nothing's wrong with it," he said. "But the problem is, Tammy should be doing those things *with* you. She isn't. Haven't you noticed?"

"Of course I've noticed." Tessa was growing less patient by the minute. "But we spend time together."

"Do you?" Alex stared at her. "Seems like

every time I call, Tammy's up in her room asleep or resting. Don't you think it's weird?''

"Not particularly," Tessa answered honestly. "I went through a phase like that a couple of years ago myself. She just needs a little space." Tessa knew the words were a lie the minute she said them. Her "I want to be alone" phase ended before she was fourteen, and even at its worst, she hadn't spent anywhere near the number of hours shut up in her bedroom as Tammy did.

But Tessa was suddenly angry. After the scene today with Doreen and all the guilt her unacceptable and shameful feelings for Alex made her feel, she didn't think it was fair of him to sit here and give her a third degree. "And I don't like what you're implying."

"I'm not implying anything," he retorted.

"Bull." Tessa tossed her napkin on the table. She hadn't eaten one bite of her dinner. "I'm not stupid, you know. In effect, you're accusing me of using my sister, of having a good time with her toys and her boyfriend."

"I never said that!" he yelped.

"You didn't have to." Tessa slid out of the booth and snatched up her purse. "I think I'd better go. Happy birthday, Alex."

The tears didn't start until she'd pulled out of the parking lot. Tessa blinked hard to keep them from rolling down her cheeks. Her head spun from the emotions pulling her in a dozen different directions. Guilt, anger, sadness, self-pity, disappointment . . .

all of them warred and fought and jockeyed for position inside her.

Guilt won. Guilt always did. Thanks, Mom.

Tessa sighed and swiped at a tear as she slowed for a red light. It had been a real treat of a day. First Doreen and her sob story about having to give "it" away because it cried all the time. And now this—Alex telling her that she was bad news for her own sister.

The awful thing was, one part of her actually believed she was, and always would be, bad news. Tessa knew she was being stupid, that she was giving in to self-pity and being pathetic, but she couldn't fight the feeling off. Deep inside her the old insecurities came back with a vengeance. Maybe she was damaged somehow. Maybe she was one of those awful people doomed to bring nothing but pain and destruction upon their families. Maybe Doreen had been right to give her away. Maybe Tammy's weird behavior really was her fault. Maybe Tammy secretly resented her coming here. . . .

But what the heck did Alex expect her to do? It wasn't like Tammy was the easiest person in the world to get along with. Tessa eased on the brakes and turned into the main road leading to the exclusive housing development where the Mercers lived. She had to get herself under control. She didn't want to run into any of the Mercers when she was like this. Especially not Tammy.

When she pulled into the driveway, she saw that neither Harold nor Doreen's car was in the open garage. Sighing in relief, she sat for a few moments, pulling herself together. Maybe she ought to go home.

Tessa straightened her spine. It might be a good idea. The summer wasn't over yet. She could still get a job, earn a few bucks for the coming semester at college. See her friends. She'd missed her friends. Most of them would still be in L.A. The more she thought about it, the more the idea appealed to her.

Deep in thought, she climbed out of the car and walked slowly up the walkway. Surely her parents would understand. Tessa pulled out the house key, unlocked the door, and stepped inside.

Her mom and dad weren't unreasonable, all she had to do was tell them the truth. She frowned as she put Tammy's car keys down on the table. But how? How could she tell them that it wasn't working out? She had nothing specific to say against Doreen and Tammy. The Mercers had been nice to her.

Just tell them that you're miserable, a little voice whispered from the back of her mind. Tessa tried to ignore it, but it was hard. Today had been one really lousy day. She knew that if her parents knew how she felt, they'd give her permission to leave. But she felt bad about even thinking of leaving. It seemed so . . . so . . . disloyal to her sister.

She glanced up the staircase. The house was as silent as a tomb. That's what this house reminded her of, a tomb. Disloyal or not, it would be better for everyone if she left. The worst that could happen would be that her parents would make her join them in Mexico for the duration of the summer. That was nothing to be depressed about.

Tessa turned and started down the hall toward the family room. It wasn't that late; her parents would still be awake.

She was reaching for the phone when the doorbell rang.

She frowned and hurried back out to the hall, wondering who would be visiting at this time of night. As Tessa pulled the door open it flashed through her mind that her mother would kill her for yanking open a door after dark without knowing who stood on the other side. Her jaw gaped in surprise when she saw Alex.

He smiled sheepishly. "Hi," he said softly. "Can I come in?"

Confused, Tessa stared at him. "Uh, yeah, sure. Do you want to see Tammy? She might still be awake. It's not that late."

Alex shook his head as he stepped inside. "I came to see you."

"Why?"

"Can we go outside on the patio and talk?" he asked, glancing up the stairway. "I don't want to be interrupted."

"Sure." Tessa led the way outside. A light summer breeze was wafting in from the ocean, filling the air with the scent of flowers. Overhead, the stars twinkled brightly against a black velvet sky. If Tessa hadn't been so confused and miserable, it would be the perfect romantic spot.

"I think I owe you an apology," Alex said. He sat down on one of the loungers. Tessa took the one opposite him so that they sat facing each other. The patio lights were on, so they could see one another's faces.

"No, you don't," she replied. "Everything you said was true. My being here isn't good for Tammy—or for me, for that matter. That's why I've decided to leave. I was just getting ready to call my parents when you showed up."

Alex's face fell. "Don't do that. Don't go. I was way out of line tonight. I was in a lousy mood because Tammy had flaked again and I took it out on you. You're not to blame because Tammy wants to play hermit all the time. Even if you weren't here, she'd be doing the same thing."

"But if I wasn't here, she'd at least feel guilty about it. Besides . . ." Tessa paused and took a deep breath. "That's not the only reason I want to go."

"Is something wrong?" he asked quietly. "I mean, have the Mercers been giving you a hard time?"

Tessa didn't know how to explain it to him; the fact was, she didn't even know how to explain it to herself. But she had to say something. "No," she blurted, "they've been real nice. They're real generous and they're not strict at all or anything. It's just that . . . that—" She broke off, not knowing how to describe the cold emptiness that had settled in her gut during this awful day and refused to go away. Heart-to-heart chats could do that to you. Maybe there were some truths it was better not to know. "I don't know. Maybe I'm just home-sick for my folks," she finished lamely.

Alex looked down at the ground. "I don't want you to go, Tessa."

"That's not what you were hinting earlier," she replied. She could feel herself softening, feel herself desperately wanting to stay, and realizing why this was so made her feel really lousy. If she agreed to stay, it would be for one reason and one reason only: Alex.

"I was a jerk earlier," he said. "I didn't mean any of those things I said to you. I was mad at Tammy, not you."

"You really care about her, don't you?" Tessa said softly. "That's why you were so bent out of shape when she didn't show."

Alex leaned back against the lounger and shut his eyes. "Maybe. I don't know. Sometimes I don't know how I feel about her at all."

"But you two have been together a long time," Tessa pointed out.

"Since ninth grade," Alex mumbled.

"But Tammy told me you'd only gone together two years," Tessa said. "Which is it? Two or four?"

Alex laughed softly. "I had a huge crush on her all the way through junior high. Then in ninth grade we became friends. We didn't start going to-gether till the beginning of our junior year, but it seems like I've known her forever. Maybe that's why I get so bugged when I see the way she's acting now.''

"That's why I should leave," Tessa murmured. "I don't think I'm good for Tammy."

Alex sat up. "That's where you're wrong, Tessa. You *are* good for her. In a few days or a few weeks she might need you more than she's ever needed anyone. God knows your mother or Harold don't have a clue."

"A clue about what?" Tessa didn't know what he was talking about. "What do you mean by that?"

Alex waved his hand in the air. "I don't want to talk about it yet. I might be full of hot air. I've got to talk to some experts before I say anything else. But I want you to promise me you won't go. For Tammy's sake, you've got to stay."

"Why?"

"I can't tell you yet," Alex said earnestly. "I don't know if I'm right. But you've got to trust me on this one."

"In case my sister needs me?"

"Right. And because I need you, too." He leaned forward and brushed his lips across hers.

Tessa knew she should stop him, she knew that this was her sister's boyfriend, but she could no more stop herself from kissing him back than she could stop the earth from spinning around the sun.

CHAPTER
FIVE

July 6

Dear Diary,
I don't know how I should feel after what hap-
pened last night. I mean, it was only a friendly
kiss, but I can't help feeling kind of guilty. Alex
is Tammy's boyfriend, not mine. But darn it, she
treats him like the invisible man. What does she
expect, that he'll put up with her prima donna
act for the rest of his life? Alex is a great guy.

"You've got a phone call. But you'll have to take
it downstairs on the other line."

Tessa jumped as Doreen's voice came through
her closed bedroom door. "Okay, I'll be right
there." She hurriedly shoved her diary into the
drawer and dashed out of her bedroom.

The family room was empty when she came
charging in, so she didn't slow her steps as she

lunged for the phone, hoping, of course, that it was Alex. "Hello."

"Hi, honey," her mother said. "I'm sorry to call so early, but I tried calling last night and there was no answer."

"Hi, Mom," Tessa replied. "You should have left a message on the answering machine, I'd have called you back."

"That's okay, dear. How are you? Are you taking all your vitamins? You know, it's real important that you take them every day. I don't want you getting run down."

"I'm taking my vitamins, Mom," Tessa hedged. Actually meals were so erratic around this house, half of the time she forgot them. "How's the shoot going?"

"Just fine, honey," Lorna said cheerfully, but Tessa detected a tone in her mother's voice that didn't ring true.

"Are you sure?" she asked, frowning at the phone.

"Positive," Lorna replied firmly. "Your daddy and I are just fine. Are you eating right? Getting plenty of fruit and vegetables?"

Tessa rolled her eyes at the ceiling. Why did her mother always treat her like a half-witted two-year-old? "I'm eating just fine, Mom." Again, that was a fib. She'd eaten tons of junk food and enjoyed every bite in the weeks she'd been here. "How's Dad?"

"He wanted me to remind you to be sure and take your vitamin E," Lorna said. "It retards the aging process, you know, and helps the body heal. Have you been getting enough sleep? I wondered where you were last night. It was pretty late when I called.''

''What time did you call?''

There was a pause. ''Well, it was around eight-thirty,'' Lorna muttered. ''I guess it wasn't all that late. But you know that you need lots of sleep. You get run down if you don't take care of yourself.''

Just then Tessa heard a noise. Still holding the phone to her ear, she turned and saw her sister leaning against the door frame, grinning. But Tessa wasn't concerned about her sister now; she was worried about her mom. Lorna might be a good actress, but Tessa could tell by her voice when she was worried about something. ''Are you sure you're all right? You sound kinda funny.''

''You're imagining things.'' Lorna laughed, but to Tessa's ears it sounded a little forced. ''I'm just fine and so is Daddy.''

''There's no trouble on the shoot, is there?'' Tessa persisted. Darn it, she didn't like it when her parents tried to hide things from her.

''Absolutely not,'' Lorna said firmly. ''Daddy and I were just a little concerned about you, that's all. Is everything going okay? Are you having a good time?''

''Yeah, Mom. I'm having a great time.'' Tessa smiled at Tammy as she spoke.

''Okay, honey. I'll call again in a couple of days.''

''I'm sure you will,'' Tessa muttered as she hung

up the phone. She glanced at her sister. "How much of that did you hear?"

"All of it." Tammy laughed. "Man, your mom sure gives you the third degree."

"Tell me about it." Tessa sighed. "I think I'm the only kid on the face of the earth whose parents went to every PTA meeting, back-to-school night, Brownie troop meeting, and volleyball meet. As a matter of fact, my dad videotaped most of those."

Tammy giggled. "You're kidding."

"Nope. For our final game last year, my dad showed up with a whole camera crew."

"Wow." Tammy looked genuinely impressed.

"Yup, it had to rank as one of the most humiliating moments of my entire life. Especially as our team was getting beat three to fourteen." Tessa couldn't help grinning at the memory. Even though at the time she could have cheerfully wrung her father's neck. "There we were getting whipped by Garfield and I look up and Daddy's got a bunch of his buddies from the studio setting up and filming the whole thing. He told me the guys owed him a favor and that as this was my last game, he wanted a record of it. Geez, he's videotaped or filmed my whole life, including some really embarrassing potty-training sequences."

Tammy burst into giggles again, and Tessa suddenly realized that this was one of the few times she'd ever seen her sister laugh. "Anyway, my folks are a pain in the neck, but they are five hundred miles away. For once, I'm not going to have my summer ruined. And by the way, What are you doing up so early?''

''I couldn't sleep,'' Tammy replied. She sauntered into the room and plopped down on the couch. ''So how did it go last night? Did Alex have a good birthday?''

''I think he had a nice time,'' Tessa said hesitantly. ''He came back here to see you, but you were asleep when we got home.'' There was no need to tell Tammy about her and Alex's fight, or about the real reason he'd come to the Mercer house. ''What's on the agenda for today?''

Tammy yawned. ''I thought I'd just lie around the pool. But if there's anything special you want to do, you can use the car.''

At that moment Doreen came bustling into the room, dressed in an elegant white sheath and putting on a pair of gold earrings. ''I'm just on my way out,'' she announced. ''There's some shrimp salad in the fridge and I've left some cash on the front table if you girls want to go out or order in a pizza.''

''Does that mean you won't be home for dinner?'' Tammy asked archly.

But Doreen didn't seem to notice her daughter's sarcasm. ''Probably not. There's a board meeting for the charity guild this morning. Then I've got a luncheon scheduled with the Friends of the Arts Council, and after that, I'll probably join Harold at the club for drinks.'' She smiled, threw them a wave, and started for the door.

"Aren't you curious about what we'll be doing today?" Tammy called.

But Doreen either didn't hear, or didn't think the question worth answering. Tessa turned from watching the empty doorway where the woman had disappeared and looked at her sister. Tammy's eyes had a bright sheen to them, as though she were struggling to hold back the tears.

Tammy caught her glance. "You see," she said bitterly. "You didn't miss a damned thing by being given away. I wish to hell she'd have given me away, too." With that, she jumped to her feet and ran out of the room.

Tessa started after her. "Tammy, wait," she yelled. But like her mother, Tammy kept right on going. A moment later Tessa heard the door of her sister's room slam shut.

Tessa spent the next few days enjoying herself. She went to the movies with Jeremy and Joleen. She did the mall a couple of times with a group of Joleen's friends and had a good time, though she didn't buy anything. And she drove Tammy's car. A lot.

All in all, it was a great way to spend the summer except for two things; Tammy and Alex. Her sister still spent far too much time shut in her room and Alex hadn't called since that night he'd kissed her.

On Friday afternoon, as Tessa was packing a beach bag for a party she and Tammy were going to that evening, she glanced at her sister and asked, "Is Alex going to be there tonight?"

"Sure." Tammy continued staring at herself in the mirror, dabbing at her cheeks with blush. "Why wouldn't he be?"

"I just wondered, that's all." Tessa carefully folded a beach towel and tucked it into the big bag. "He hasn't been around much this week."

"He's called every day," Tammy said. "His boss is on vacation, so he's put in a lot of hours at the video store. I wish he'd quit that crummy little job. It's not like he needs the cash. His parents are loaded."

Tessa found that she was rather hurt. Alex had called every day and hadn't asked to speak to her even once. Then she caught herself. Why should he want to talk to her? He was Tammy's guy. "You about ready?"

"Just a minute." Tammy disappeared into her own room and came out carrying an oblong object wrapped in a brown paper bag. Tessa watched her tuck it into the bag.

"Okay." She smiled brightly. "Now I'm ready."

"We'd better leave a note for Doreen and Harold," Tessa muttered. She knew what was in the bag, but she didn't have the guts to say anything.

Tammy snorted. "Why? They'll be at the country club schmoozing with their friends half the night. Take my word for it, they won't even notice we're gone."

• • •

It took a good half hour to reach the coast. For once, Tammy drove and Tessa found herself almost resenting the fact that her sister was behind the wheel. Joleen was just getting out of her little red Toyota when they pulled up in the parking lot next to her.

"Hi," Joleen called. "This ought to be a fabulous party. There's already tons of people here."

"Good," Tammy said as the twins climbed out of the car. Tessa noticed that her sister grabbed the beach bag but didn't bother to lock the car door. "I hope it doesn't get cold. Did Jeremy bring his scanner?"

Joleen nodded and the girls hurried down to the sand, where over a dozen kids were grouped around a fire pit. For the next few minutes Tessa was too busy greeting everyone to pay much attention to her sister's activities. By the time she turned around to look for her, she saw Tammy and Alex, whom Tessa hadn't even seen arrive, heading off down the beach.

"Thank goodness those two are going off to do some talking," Joleen muttered as she came over and plopped down on the beach towel next to Tessa. "I was getting worried about them."

"Worried? Why?" Tessa asked. She knew it was stupid, but the fact that Alex had not even said hello to her really hurt.

"Because Tammy's been acting like a hermit lately." Joleen idly picked up a handful of sand and let it scatter in the evening breeze. "And I'd hate to see her and Alex break up. They're such a cute couple. I thought that maybe Alex was getting fed up with her sitting at home all the time.''

''Well, uh, maybe she likes being at home.'' The moment the words were out, Tessa winced inwardly. Talk about lame.

Joleen laughed. ''Are you kidding? Tammy's no more a homebody than I am. She just doesn't like to go anywhere where she can't drink. Why do you think she won't go with us to the mall or the movies or even over to someone's house if they're likely to have nosy parents?''

Tessa said nothing. An awful idea began to take hold in her mind. Was that the reason Tammy was always in her room? Sure, sometimes she could smell wine on her breath, but Tessa honestly hadn't thought she drank that much. Was her sister really drinking so much that she'd rather stay in that empty house than go out and be with her friends? No, that was crazy. She couldn't believe it.

''Thank God you came along when you did,'' Joleen continued. ''At least now Tammy doesn't get behind the wheel when she's plastered.''

''What do you mean by that?''

Joleen laughed. ''Well, she had a couple of close calls. But now, she's got you to do the driving.''

''I'd like to think she likes me for more than my driving skills,'' Tessa murmured. But she wondered. It seemed like the only times she and Tammy went anywhere together, she did end up driving home. Was that what she was to her sister? A convenience? No, it wasn't true. She and Tammy had gotten close.

Or had they?

Joleen stood up and dusted the sand off her jeans. ''I think I'll go see what Tom's up to. He broke up with Darlene a couple of weeks ago.'' She flashed Tessa an impish grin. ''I think he needs a shoulder to cry on.''

Tessa nodded absently. She glanced around and saw that the party was in full swing. Kids were milling around everywhere. The noise level was so loud you could barely hear the waves crashing against the beach. Hard rock blasted from a portable CD player, a couple of guys were yelling at the top of their lungs as they played Frisbee, and someone's dog was barking its head off.

Tessa got up and walked down toward the water. She glanced back to make sure that no one was watching her and then turned in the direction of some rocks up the beach. She had a lot of thinking to do.

She found a relatively peaceful spot a little ways up the beach and sat down next to a craggy outcrop. As she watched the sun set she wondered exactly what kind of relationship she did have with her sister. Tessa stared at the setting sun and played games with her conscience. She kept thinking about everything Alex had said at the restaurant. Just how close were she and Tammy? The question haunted her. Sure, they spent a lot of time talking, but it was never about anything important. They chatted about clothes and movies and gossiped, but they never talked about anything serious. Like why did Tammy spend so much time shut up in her room and how much was she really drinking? Tessa sighed. She didn't think her sister was ready for the funny farm or anything. Tammy was just experimenting with booze. Lots of kids did that.

Then why did Tessa feel like such a snake? She wrapped her arms around her drawn-up knees and hugged herself tightly as an ugly truth crept into her thoughts. *You hypocrite. The truth is, you like the situation just the way it is.* No. She shut her eyes, determined to push the hideous idea out of her mind. But it kept coming right back.

"No," she mumbled. "I'm not a hypocrite." But it was so convenient just to slip on one of Tammy's great outfits, take the car keys, and head out, rather than pitch a fit and make her sister come with her.

A chill wind blasted in off the Pacific, bringing with it a faint spray of water off the waves. Tessa stood up and dusted the sand off her fanny. Maybe it would help if she talked to Alex.

Tessa headed farther up the beach, away from the party. This section of the coast was fairly rugged and the waves were crashing so hard against the sand that she didn't see or hear anything until she was practically on top of them. Tessa stood in the shadow of a rock and frowned. Talk about a case of bad timing. From the looks of things, Alex and Tammy were having a doozy of an argument. They were on the other side of the rocks, facing each other. Her sister's face was twisted in anger; Alex's mouth was a flat, grim line.

Alex shoved some papers he was holding toward

Tammy, but she slapped at his fingers. "I don't want that crap," she yelled. There was a hysterical note in her voice. Tessa wondered if she should go back to the party or stay and see what the heck was wrong.

"The hell you don't." Alex waved the papers under her nose. "At least read them."

"Buzz off." Tammy slapped his fingers again, this time hard enough that the papers fell and were caught by the wind. "There's nothing wrong with me. I can handle it. I don't need any help. Mind your own damned business." Then she turned and ran, heading along the other side of the big rock where Tessa stood and not even noticing her standing there.

"Alex?" Tessa hurried over to him. "What's going on?"

For a moment he didn't answer. Then he dropped to his knees and began to pick up the scattered pages.

"Alex?" Tessa prompted him. "I asked you what's going on? Is Tammy okay?"

He got up, his expression hard and angry. "Fat lot you care," he snarled.

"What's that supposed to mean?" She was starting to get a little angry herself.

"Exactly what it says." He turned his back on her and faced the ocean. "You've been having a real good time, haven't you? You drive her car, you wear her clothes, you see all her friends." He laughed bitterly. "And you even come after her boyfriend."

Tessa exploded. She grabbed his arm and tugged hard enough to spin him around to face her. "Look, I don't know what's going on, but I'm sick and tired of you picking on me every time you're upset with Tammy. This is the second time it's happened and I've had it."

Alex narrowed his eyes. "You've had it? Maybe I've had it, too—with both of you." He started walking up the beach.

But Tessa wasn't giving up that easily. Something was going on here, something that concerned her sister, and she had a right to know what it was. This wasn't just some boyfriend-girlfriend fight she'd interrupted.

"Oh no, you don't," she yelled, keeping pace with his long strides. "You're going to tell me what happened back there and why my sister is so upset."

"Because I told her the truth," he snapped, "and she didn't like hearing it."

"What truth?" Tessa practically had to run to keep up with him now. "What are you talking about?"

Alex stopped. Tessa skidded to a halt beside him. "Don't you get it?" he said, using a tone that indicated he thought she was a half-wit. "Tammy's got a problem."

"You mean her experimenting with alcohol?" Tessa liked that phrase. It didn't sound as bad as the other word that had popped into her head.

"Is that what you call it? 'Experimenting'?" Alex stared hard at her.

Unable to meet his intense gaze, Tessa shrugged and looked out at the ocean. The way he was looking at her made her feel funny. Kind of guilty. "Well, yeah," she said hesitantly. "I mean, lots of kids play around with booze. It's not like she's doing vodka or hard stuff all the time. She just has a little wine."

"A little wine!" he said, his tone incredulous. "Are you deaf, dumb, and blind? She doesn't just chug back Mommy and Daddy's leftover dinner wine. She pours the stuff down her throat like it's water."

"You're overreacting, Alex," Tessa began. She wasn't sure she wanted to hear any more. "It's not like she can't stop, you know."

"It's exactly like she can't stop," he insisted. He pulled the crumbled papers out of his pocket and thrust them toward Tessa. "Here, read these. Then you'll know."

"Know what?" Tessa demanded.

"That Tammy's an alcoholic." Alex ran his hands over his face. "And what's worse, you and I both have been helping her to stay that way, too."

"You're saying it's my fault that she drinks?" Tessa yelped.

"Who knows why she drinks?" Alex replied. "I'm not a shrink. I don't know why anyone decides to crawl into a bottle instead of living. But I do know one thing—neither of us has been helping her. Especially you. She's gotten worse since you've come. Much worse. She's barely been out of the house since June."

Tessa was dumbfounded by his accusations. But before she could protest, Tom came running up. "You guys had better make tracks," he yelled. "The cops are on the way. Jeremy picked it up on the scanner."

"Hell," Alex muttered. "Is Tammy plastered?" he asked Tom.

Tom shrugged. "She's working on it. I don't think she's too far gone yet, but if I were you, I wouldn't let her drive."

Without another word, Tessa and Alex followed Tom back to the party. Tammy was sitting on the beach towel, a bottle of wine between her legs. The other kids were packing up and heading toward the parking lot.

"Well, well, well," Tammy singsonged when she spotted Alex and Tessa. "What have you two been up to?" She giggled at her own wit and burped.

Alex didn't bother to answer. He picked up the wine bottle and tossed it into a trash can.

"Hey, that's mine," Tammy protested. She struggled to get to her feet, her attention on the trash can, but Alex grabbed her arms and stopped her as she lunged toward the huge green container. "Let go," Tammy snarled. "I want my stuff back."

"You've had enough," he said harshly. "The cops are on the way. So unless you want to spend the night in the drunk tank, I'd suggest you get moving."

"Alex, you don't have to be so rough with her," Tessa protested.

Alex shot her a glare. "Would you rather I leave her here for the police to find?" He turned and began pulling her none too gently over the sand. Tammy stumbled and Tessa automatically started to help her sister, but Alex shook his head. "I'll get her to the car, you get the stuff together. We've got to get out of here."

Tammy was surprisingly docile on the way home. She talked little; mainly she just closed her eyes and leaned her head back against the seat. Tessa wondered how she had gotten so drunk so fast. Then she realized that Tammy had probably been drinking before they left for the beach. After that scene with Alex, it had probably taken only a few good belts to push her over the edge.

Tessa drove as fast as she dared and breathed a heartfelt sigh of relief when she pulled into the driveway and saw that the Mercers were still out.

"Come on," she said to Tammy. "Let's get you inside and up to bed before your parents get home."

Tammy belched and stumbled as she got out of the car. "No sweat. They won't be home for hours. I don't think they like it here either."

"You're talking nonsense." Tessa took her sister's arm and guided her toward the front door. She hoped none of the neighbors were watching because Tammy was weaving like a palm frond in a hurricane.

Balancing one arm around her sister and digging into her jeans for the house key, she managed to get the door open and both of them inside. Tessa tossed the keys onto the table. "Can you make it upstairs?"

Tammy yawned, lunged for the newel post, and put her foot on the first stair. But she missed her footing and swayed backward. Tessa grabbed her, put her arms around her firmly and marched her up the stairs.

She got Tammy into her room and dumped her on the bed. Tammy closed her eyes and either fell asleep or passed out. As Tessa stood looking down at her sister she wasn't sure which. What should she do? If Tammy was passed out, maybe she should turn her onto her side. Tessa had read somewhere that people who'd had too much to drink shouldn't sleep on their backs. If they threw up, they might choke on it. Or was she thinking of newborn babies? They weren't supposed to sleep on their backs either. She grabbed Tammy's shoulders and pushed her onto her side. Tammy moaned softly, but didn't wake up. Tessa snatched up a pillow and tucked it firmly against Tammy's spine, propping her on her side.

Kneeling by the bed, she unlaced Tammy's shoes and pulled them off. She decided to let Tammy sleep in her clothes. There was no way she could get those tight jeans off without her sister's cooperation. She pulled the bedspread over her and flicked off the light.

Closing the door quietly, Tessa came down the

hall, sat down on the top stair, and pulled the crumpled papers out of her pocket.

Tessa stared at them, her expression grim. She took a deep breath and began to read. The brochures didn't give a lot of specific details, but there was enough information in them to send her stomach plummeting to her toes.

When she finished reading, she sat frozen, too numb to move as the truth seeped into her with a finality she couldn't deny. She felt like someone had punched her in the gut or tossed her on a spinning merry-go-round without giving her a chance to buy a ticket.

She glanced at the brochures that had fallen onto the carpet. She didn't want to believe it was true, but that would be like trying to deny that the earth rotated around the sun. Like it or not, she had to face the truth.

Basically, there were several criteria by which to judge whether or not someone had a problem with alcohol. The criteria for judging whether a teenager had that particular problem were a little different from the criteria used for adults. Teenagers, after all, generally didn't have full-time jobs to lose or families to abuse. But if their social habits changed, if every event in their life began to revolve around access to alcohol, well, then they had a problem.

Hell, she thought miserably. The darned brochure could have been written about her sister. Bottom line was that Alex was right. Tammy had a real problem.

Tessa shut her eyes briefly, not wanting to see

the ugly words on the front of the crinkled brochure. But the image refused to go away. The big red letters were seared on the back of her eyelids.

And the words were horrible.

Teenage Alcoholism.

Tessa felt the tears well up in her eyes. She blinked hard, but that didn't make the truth disappear.

Tammy was an alcoholic.

CHAPTER SIX

Dear Diary,
I didn't sleep much last night. After reading that
darned brochure, how could anyone sleep? I guess
I must have been in shock or something, because
I sat there on the steps until I heard Doreen and
Harold's car pull in. Funny, though, last night
was the first time I realized how much the Mer-
cers drink, too. When I heard them coming in, I
hightailed it to my room. But I could hear every-
thing from downstairs. Doreen was looped and I
think Harold was, too. They were giggling like a
couple of teenagers, and when I stuck my head
out and peeked over the railing, Harold was
weaving as he walked. I heard Doreen say she
wanted to "check on the girls," but Harold said,
"Don't be silly, they're okay." Then they went
into the den for a "nightcap." Maybe this is

where Tammy gets it from? Heck, I don't know. Right now I don't know much of anything. I'm worried about Tammy and my mom sounded funny on the phone yesterday, so I'm uptight about my parents, too, and to top it all, Alex called a few minutes ago and wants me to meet him for breakfast. From the way he sounded, I don't think this qualifies as a date.

Tessa glanced at her watch, saw that she had to meet Alex in fifteen minutes, and put her diary back in the drawer. Today she hadn't worried about how she looked or what she wore; she'd just thrown on a pair of old jeans and a T-shirt.

She grabbed her purse and went downstairs, moving quietly since everyone else was still asleep. She wondered briefly if she ought to leave a note, then decided it didn't matter.

Tammy, whom she'd checked on several times during the night, was sound asleep and the Mercers wouldn't care where she'd gone anyway. Tessa wondered again why the Mercers had wanted her to spend the summer here in the first place. Doreen certainly wasn't into playing "mommy," even with the daughter she'd kept. So she certainly wasn't interested in bonding with the kid she'd given away. Tessa frowned as she opened the front door and stepped outside. Maybe bringing her here had just been a whim. Or maybe it had been Tammy's idea. Maybe it didn't matter. She was here now and she wasn't going to leave until she did something to help her sister. Maybe they hadn't gotten as close as Tessa would have liked, but that didn't matter. Tessa's parents had taught her that you didn't walk away from a relative who needed help.

A mist had drifted in during the night, turning the morning a dull gray, much like her mood. She climbed into the car, put the key in the ignition, and pulled out of the driveway.

Ten minutes later she walked into the coffee shop and looked around for Alex. He was sitting at a booth in the corner, his expression grim. He spotted her then and waved.

Tessa slid in across from him. "Hi," she said.

"Hi." He stirred his coffee. "You want something to eat?"

"No, I'm not very hungry this morning."

The waitress brought another menu. "I'll just have some coffee," Tessa told her.

"Tammy okay?" he asked.

"She was sleeping when I left."

"Good." He glanced out the window and then down at the table. "Look, uh, I'm sorry about everything I said last night."

"Are you?" Tessa asked. He didn't look a bit sorry. He looked angry and ready to bite someone's head off. Well, good, they were even, then. She was pretty ticked off herself.

"I said I was, didn't I?" he said defensively. "I was way out of line, okay?"

Tessa waited until the waitress put her coffee in front of her and then she leaned across the table. "It's not okay," she hissed. "I felt like pond scum last night because of the things you said to me."

"Did you read the brochure?" he challenged.

"Of course I did," she snapped. "And that only made me feel worse. You're right, she does have a problem. And thanks to you, I spent most of the night awake and feeling it was all my fault."

"I didn't mean to dump it all on you," he mumbled. "I've got to take some of the blame, too."

"That's big of you." She stirred cream into her coffee.

"You're in a lousy mood this morning."

"What did you expect? Sweetness and light?" Tessa sighed. "Look, this isn't helping. It's my sister that's got trouble, not me."

"But one of the reasons she has this problem is because of the way both of us have been letting her get away with it." Alex reached across the table and laid his hand on Tessa's. "Do you know what an 'enabler' is?"

"I've heard the word," Tessa replied. She gently pulled her hand away. She had enough on her conscience now, she wasn't going to add to it by playing touchy-feely with her sister's boyfriend. But Alex didn't seem to notice.

"An enabler is someone who helps another person feed their addiction," he explained. "Sometimes for what they think are the best of reasons. That's what we've been doing."

"No, we haven't," Tessa protested.

"Yes, we have," he insisted. "We've covered for her. That's the worst thing we could have done. We've fixed it so she doesn't have to face the consequences of her actions. By picking up after her, by always being there to clean up her messes, we've made it easy for her to drink.''

''But what else could we have done?'' Tessa demanded. ''Let her lie on the beach half-drunk until the cops picked her up?''

''Maybe that wouldn't have been such a bad thing,'' he said. ''At least then her parents would know the truth. Maybe if she got hassled by the cops and had to spend the night in the drunk tank, she'd clean up her act.''

''I'm not even sure she's got an act to clean up,'' Tessa said angrily. She was grasping at straws, but she had to be sure. What did she and Alex know about alcoholism? Reading a brochure didn't make them experts. ''I mean, I know what the brochure said, and I'm not saying that she doesn't go overboard with the booze every now and again, but are we sure she's an alcoholic? Are we sure she can't stop drinking? That's what an alcoholic is, right. Someone who can't stop?''

Alex cocked his head to one side and regarded her thoughtfully. ''Do you know how long she's been drinking?''

Tessa shrugged. ''No. I never asked her.''

''Tammy started drinking in ninth grade,'' he said softly. ''Back then we all thought it was cool.''

''She was fourteen?'' Tessa couldn't believe it. ''But that's crazy.''

''I know it's crazy. She started sipping Harold and Doreen's leftover dinner wine when she was in ninth grade. By the time she was a sophomore, she was sneaking glasses out of bottles they left in the fridge. By the time she was a senior, she was stealing whole bottles from the pantry.''

"But didn't Doreen or Harold ever notice?"

Alex shook his head. ''Nah, like I told you before. Tammy's smart. She used to wait until she heard her mother phoning the wine order in to the liquor store, then Tammy would get on the phone and increase the order. Doreen's never around, so when the stuff was delivered, Tammy would pinch the extra bottles from the order. She'd hide them up in her room.''

"Okay, but that still doesn't prove she's an alcoholic. It might just be her way of getting back at the Mercers because they're gone all the time.''

"Good grief,'' he said disgustedly. ''Does it take a house to fall on you? Tammy can't stop. Take my word for it. I know what you're thinking, Tessa—''

"No, you don't,'' she interrupted angrily.

"Oh yes, I do,'' he shot back. ''I know because I tried to con myself the same way. You're thinking this is just a phase and that she can stop the boozing anytime she wants. But believe me, hiding your head in the sand and making excuses for her won't make the truth go away. Tammy has to drink. She's got an addiction. Telling yourself she's just playing around or experimenting or trying to get back at her parents won't make it go away.''

"But what can we do?'' Tessa cried helplessly. That was the tough part. Even if what he said was true, what could they possibly do about it? Despite her brave resolve earlier, now that they were down to it, her determination to help Tammy was wavering. Not because she didn't want to help her sister, but because she was scared. Taking on a problem this size was a big responsibility. What if they screwed up? What if they made things worse?

"For starters, we can face the truth ourselves."

"What good will that do?"

He stared at her sympathetically. Finally, he said, "If we understand what's happening to her, it might stop us from making it worse."

"But I didn't do that. All I did was try to be her friend," Tessa protested. One of the things that had kept her staring at the ceiling all night had been Alex's accusations yesterday at the beach. "Okay, so I drive her car and wear her clothes, big deal. I didn't ask for any of that, Tammy insisted."

"Right," he said gently. "She insisted. Did you ever stop to ask yourself why?"

"Because I'm her sister, that's why."

Alex sipped his coffee. "That's part of it, sure. But Tammy had other reasons."

"What other reasons?"

"If you were out driving around in her car, you wouldn't be home watching what she did, would you?" he pointed out. "And if you were wearing her clothes and hanging out with her friends, you wouldn't complain to Doreen or your own parents that your darling sister was totally ignoring you, wouldn't you? Face it, Tessa, Tammy got stuck with you for the summer and she didn't want that to interfere with her boozing it up. So she conned you the only way she knew how. She gave you everything you wanted and you lapped it up like a starving kitten.''

His words hurt. Because deep inside, she knew they were true. One part of her had known something was going on, something weird and calculating and too ugly to face. She swallowed the sudden lump in her throat. ''Maybe I did, but I never wanted to hurt her.''

''I know.'' He smiled sadly. ''Neither did I. I'm as guilty as you are. That's one of the reasons I lashed out at you so hard yesterday. Tammy ducking out this summer made things easy for me, too.''

''How?'' Tessa was totally confused now.

''Because it meant that I could be with you,'' he said simply. He looked down at his coffee cup. ''I really like you. I guess you know that, huh?''

''Maybe,'' she said slowly. What did he want her to admit? That she was such a worm she wanted her sister's boyfriend? But the truth was, he was right. She did like Alex. She knew he liked her, too. ''I guess I sort of suspected you really liked me.''

''Yeah, I do. And not just as a friend, either.''

It was out in the open now, but that didn't make it easier for Tessa. Her emotions were one big messy jumble. Elation that he felt the same way as she did, guilt that the one boy she'd ever met that she really, really liked belonged to her own sister, and pain that in finding him, she'd also found out her sister had a problem that could ruin her life.

"So I went along with it, too," he continued honestly. "Just like I've gone along with everything else Tammy wanted for the past couple of years. Like I said, I'm as guilty as you are. I've covered for her plenty of times. But she's guilty, too. She's been using you."

"So what do we do now?" Tessa asked.

"I'm not sure," he said. "But we've got to do something. She can't go on drinking like this."

Tessa agreed. "Last night I kept thinking that once I'm gone, she'll start driving again. The idea gave me nightmares."

"I know. But you're not going until September. We'll come up with something."

"What? I can't run around behind her hiding her booze," Tessa pointed out.

"That wouldn't make any difference anyway," he said. "She'd find a way. Tammy's really addicted to the stuff; she'll get it somehow. She's got tons of cash. Her parents are always giving her money. Plus she's got a bank account of her own and credit cards. She can always find someone to buy booze for her."

"So what do you suggest?" Tessa stared at him expectantly, desperately hoping that he would come up with something.

"The way I see it," Alex said slowly, "there's only one thing we can do. I'm not even sure it'll work, but it's the only idea I can come up with."

"Well," she demanded, "what is it?"

Alex took a deep breath and sat up ramrod straight. "You've got to snitch on her. You've got to tell the Mercers everything. The only people who can help her now are her parents.''

Tessa thought Alex had lost his mind. Why should she be the one to do the dirty work? Why couldn't he tell them? But Alex had calmly pointed out that they'd be much more likely to believe someone who lived with Tammy. She hated to admit it, but he did have a point. Still, she thought as she drove home, she wasn't sure it was a good idea. She and the Mercers weren't exactly close. But she'd promised Alex she'd think about it. Meanwhile part of her was hoping that after the scene last night at the beach, Tammy might take it upon herself to face her addiction. What the heck, stranger things had happened. She'd see how her sister was this morning. Maybe she herself could bring the subject up in a tactful way and see how Tammy responded.

When she arrived home, she discovered that the Mercers had already gotten up and gone out. There was a note on the kitchen counter from Doreen. She and Harold were having brunch on a friend's yacht.

Tessa shoved the note to one side and entered the family room. She stared at the phone, wishing briefly that she could call her parents. But that wouldn't do her any good. They were hundreds of miles away. Besides, if they knew the truth about the situation, they'd have her out of here in a fast minute. She didn't want that. Whatever happened, she was going to help her sister.

She heard footsteps coming heavily down the

stairs. "Tammy," she called, jumping up and running out into the hall. "Are you okay?"

"Where are they?" Tammy asked, and Tessa knew she meant her parents.

"They're having brunch on a yacht with some friends," Tessa replied.

"They're probably with the Jacksons. That means they won't be back for hours." Tammy headed for the kitchen.

Tessa followed her. "You want me to make you some coffee?"

"No." Tammy went to the pantry and Tessa watched her with a sinking heart.

"It's no trouble," Tessa said desperately. "I was just going to make myself a pot. Would you like some breakfast? I'm pretty good at scrambling eggs—"

"Don't make me barf," Tammy interrupted. "And I don't want any damned coffee." She knelt down and stared at the contents of the bottom shelf. She reached inside, shoved the front bottles to one side, and pulled out one from the back.

"Don't you think it's a little early?" Tessa asked.

Tammy stood up, tucked the bottle under her arm, and glared at her sister. "What's it to you?"

"Look," Tessa tried again. "I think maybe you've got a problem here. For crying out loud, it's not even eleven o'clock and you're breaking into the wine."

"Mind your own business," Tammy snapped.

She tossed Tessa a fast glare and hurried out of the room.

Tessa stared at the empty doorway for a moment and then turned slowly to the phone mounted on the wall. She picked it up and dialed. How could she have been so blind? How could anyone not have seen what was going on with her sister? Alex answered on the second ring. Tessa didn't waste any time with pleasantries. "Alex, it's Tessa."

"Hey, what's up? Have you thought about what we talked about?"

"Are you working today?"

"Yeah, but only until five."

"Good, because I may need a little moral support this afternoon." She paused and took a deep breath. "I'm going to tell Doreen and Harold."

The Mercers didn't come home until almost three o'clock. By that time, Tessa was a nervous wreck, but she was determined to go through with it. Tammy had spent the entire day locked up in her room. Tessa knew she was in there pouring liquor down her throat.

"Hello, Tessa." Doreen smiled brightly as she and Harold stepped into the hall. "Have you had a nice day?"

"It was fine, thanks."

"Coming through, coming through." Harold pushed past his wife and Tessa. "I'm got to hurry. We've got a three-fifteen tee time at the club."

"But I need to talk to you," Tessa protested. But

she was talking to Harold's back. He'd disappeared into the study.

"Talk to us?" Doreen's perfectly made-up face creased in worry. "About what?"

Tessa hesitated. She didn't want to blurt it out standing here in the hall. "About something important."

Harold reappeared with his golf bag slung across his back. "I'll probably eat dinner at the club," he said, stopping to peck Doreen on the cheek. "Why don't you meet me there around seven; we're only playing nine holes."

"All right, dear," Doreen said.

Tessa felt like screaming. What was with these people? Were they deaf, dumb, and blind? "But I need to talk to you," she began.

"You can talk to me." Doreen cut her off and ushered Harold out the front door. She gave her husband a last wave. "I'll be there at seven." Then she turned to Tessa. "Now, why don't we go into the study and you can tell me whatever is on your mind."

After glancing up the stairwell toward Tammy's room, Tessa followed Doreen into the study. Maybe this was the way it should be. Harold wasn't exactly a candidate for stepfather of the year. Maybe it would be easier talking only to Doreen. But Tessa was still annoyed at the way the adults acted.

Folding her hands in her lap, Doreen sat down on the couch and invited Tessa to do the same.

Tessa took the chair opposite her.

"Now." Doreen smiled brightly. "What do you want to tell me?"

This close to the woman, Tessa could smell alcohol on her breath. That didn't bode well. But she was determined. "This is really hard for me," she began.

"You want to go home?" Doreen interrupted. "Is that what this is about? But that's impossible. Your parents are in Mexico."

"No." Tessa shook her head impatiently. "I don't want to go home. I want to talk to you about Tammy."

"Tammy?" Doreen looked puzzled. "But I thought you girls were getting along just fine. I haven't heard any arguing or fights."

"We *are* getting along fine," Tessa replied. "I, uh, love my sister very much."

A strange, unreadable expression flashed across Doreen's face. Then she composed herself. "Good, I'm glad to hear it. So what's your problem?"

"I don't have a problem," Tessa said softly. "Tammy does."

Doreen stared at her for a long moment. "I'm afraid I don't understand. What on earth are you saying? She's not pregnant, is she?"

"Of course not," Tessa said quickly. "But it's something that I think is just as serious and just as likely to ruin her life if she doesn't get help."

"What are you talking about?" Doreen's voice rose shrilly.

"I'm talking about Tammy's drinking," Tessa blurted out. She paused and took another deep breath. "Tammy's an alcoholic. You've got to do something about it before she drinks herself into an early grave." There, she'd said it. Now Doreen and Harold had to help.

Doreen went utterly still. For a long moment she said nothing. She simply stared at Tessa with a confused, puzzled expression on her face. "I don't think I understand," she finally said.

Tessa couldn't believe it. Didn't this woman understand English? "What do you not understand? Tammy drinks. She's addicted to alcohol. She's an alcoholic."

Doreen stood up. "I don't believe this," she said, her voice angry. "How dare you come into this house and start telling lies?"

"I'm not lying," Tessa protested. "Go upstairs and look under her bed or in her closet. You'll find the empty bottles. For goodness' sake, do you think it's normal for a seventeen-year-old girl to spend her entire life locked in her bedroom?"

"She's just moody," Doreen yelled. "She's always been that way."

"She isn't moody," Tessa shot back, angry now. "She's drinking."

"I won't listen to any more of these lies." Doreen started for the door.

"I'm not lying. The proof's right upstairs."

Doreen stopped at the doorway. "A few wine bottles wouldn't prove anything," she hissed. "All kids do a little experimenting; it's normal."

"The way Tammy drinks isn't normal," Tessa persisted. She was determined to make this woman face the truth. Her sister's life might depend on it. "Tammy can't stop. That means she's an alcoholic."

"Seventeen-year-olds do not become alcoholics," Doreen cried.

"She's been drinking since she was in the ninth grade." Tessa balled her hands into fists. She had to make her understand.

"Stop it." Doreen covered her ears with her hands. "I won't listen to another word. You don't know what it was like. You have no idea how hard I've worked to make sure we had a home. I won't let anyone ruin it. I won't, do you hear me?"

"I'm not trying to ruin anything," Tessa said earnestly. What was Doreen babbling about? They were supposed to be talking about Tammy. "I'm trying to help my sister."

"You can help her by keeping your silly ideas to yourself." Doreen pulled herself together. "Obviously, considering the way you were raised, you tend to overdramatize everything. I'm not saying that my daughter hasn't ever had a sip or two of wine, but at her age that's normal."

"Her drinking isn't normal," Tessa said. "I don't think you understand—"

"Oh, I understand all right," Doreen interrupted coldly. "And to some extent, I even sympathize with you. But you really mustn't let your jealousy get the better of you."

"Jealousy?" Tessa thought that was the most ridiculous thing she'd ever heard. Whatever feelings of resentment or jealousy she may have had of her sister evaporated weeks ago. "I don't feel that way at all."

Doreen gave her a pitying smile. "Of course you do, and I'll admit, to some extent it's probably my fault. You probably have some silly idea that I shouldn't have given you up for adoption." She laughed shrilly. "According to the psychiatrists, just about everything is the mother's fault. But nonetheless, we really can't have you saying such outrageous things about your sister. Why, Harold would be absolutely furious if I repeated the things you've told me." With that, she stalked out the door, leaving a stunned and disbelieving Tessa to stare after her.

"I don't get it," she mumbled to herself. "It's like she doesn't want to know." Slowly, still shocked despite her own knowledge that Doreen wouldn't exactly be a good candidate for mother of the year, Tessa picked up the phone and dialed Alex's number.

He must have been waiting for her call because he answered on the first ring. "Tessa?"

"Yeah, it's me."

"How'd it go?"

"Awful. She doesn't believe me."

"Damn." Alex sighed. "I was afraid of that. Hang on, I'll be right over. We've got to talk."

"Okay, I'll be waiting outside."

Tessa walked out into the hall, fully expecting to find a rampaging Tammy charging down the stairs with her claws extended toward Tessa's throat. But the house was quiet. She sighed and relaxed against the wall. Apparently, Doreen hadn't gone up and said anything to Tammy.

She was suddenly bone-tired. She glanced up the silent stairs again and then walked to the front door. There was no need to leave a note or bother telling anyone where she was going. They wouldn't care. Tammy had her booze. Doreen had her head in the sand. Obviously, that was the way everyone liked it.

Tessa stood outside and waited for Alex. He pulled up a few minutes later, leaned across the front seat of his small compact, and flipped open the door. "Get in," he ordered. "We'll go someplace quiet."

Tessa was too drained to talk. She sat quietly staring out the front window, not stirring until Alex pulled into the parking lot at the city park. Wordlessly, they got out and wandered across the velvet green grass. Some kids were kicking a soccer ball around on the other side of the field. A couple of elderly men were playing chess at one of the tables near the recreation building, and the play area was filled with toddlers enjoying the swings and slides.

They sat down under a tree. Alex gazed at her sympathetically. "Guess it was pretty rough, huh."

"You could say that." Tessa shook her head. "She didn't believe me. She accused me of being jealous and making up lies. Even when I told her to go upstairs and look under Tammy's bed for the empty bottles, she wouldn't do it."

"She doesn't want to know," Alex said. "I'm not surprised. Doreen's always been that way.

When Tammy was flunking tenth-grade English, Doreen refused to even go in and talk to the teacher. She simply won't believe anything she doesn't want to.'' He shrugged helplessly. ''It's not that she doesn't love Tammy, she does. I know it. But she's always been kinda weird, if you know what I mean. It's like she's afraid her whole life will fall apart if one little thing isn't perfect.''

''She's weird all right,'' Tessa muttered. She suddenly wished that her own mom was there. Lorna might be overprotective and too strict, but if someone tried to tell her that her daughter was in trouble, she'd not only listen, she'd move heaven and earth to do whatever she could to help. So would her dad. But they weren't here.

She and Alex were on their own. ''What are we going to do?'' she asked sadly.

''What can we do?'' He shrugged. ''I'm all out of ideas. Unless . . .''

''Unless what?'' Right now, Tessa would go for just about anything.

''Unless you want to call your folks,'' Alex suggested.

''Are you crazy? What good would that do? They don't have any pull with Doreen and Harold. I still can't even figure out why they agreed to let me come up here. It really wasn't like them at all.''

''Maybe they don't have any pull,'' Alex said hastily. ''But they can make you go home.''

''But I don't want to go home,'' Tessa pointed out. She was a little hurt. Didn't Alex want her to stay? "Besides, they're in Mexico for the summer."

"You don't get it," he said. "What I meant was they could rattle the ice queen. Your parents don't sound like the kind that want you to be around someone who is always pouring booze down her throat. You can get them to threaten to make you leave here if Doreen doesn't do something about Tammy's boozing."

"It wouldn't be a threat," Tessa replied dryly. "If they knew Tammy was a lush, they'd have me out of here in a New York minute. As a matter of fact, Doreen was so pissed at me, I wouldn't be surprised if she doesn't call them herself to tell them she's putting me on the next plane for Mexico."

CHAPTER
SEVEN

July 8

Dear Diary,
Yesterday was a really bad day. Alex and I talk a good game, but when it comes right down to it, I'm not sure anything short of locking Tammy up is going to work. It's one thing to latch onto fancy words like "intervention," but I'm not sure either of us knows exactly what it means. But Alex and I both think we can't give up. If we don't do something, Tammy's headed for real trouble. Anyway, this intervention thing was the only idea we could come up with yesterday. I guess I'd better give it my best shot. But frankly, I'm not looking forward to confronting Tammy. Whether it works or not, well, we'll see. But I've got to know I tried.

Tessa sighed, closed her diary, and shoved it into the drawer. Swinging her legs off the bed, she got up and started toward the bathroom.

There was no point in putting it off. She had to face her sister sooner or later. When she'd gotten home yesterday afternoon, Tammy had already been holed up in her room. Luckily, Doreen and Harold had been out until late and Tessa hadn't had to see either of them. The thought of facing Doreen after their little chat yesterday made her half-sick to her stomach.

For a moment Tessa was overcome with homesickness. Right now she'd give anything to be with her own mom and dad. They'd know what to do. They'd know how to handle something like this. But they weren't here. She was. Resentment, hot and fierce, welled up in her stomach. Why did she have to deal with this? Why was it her responsibility? But the feeling faded as quickly as it had come. Tammy was her sister, and right now, whether she knew it or not, she needed help. If Tessa didn't do it, who would?

Suddenly the bedroom door burst open and slammed against the wall. Tessa stopped in her tracks as her sister charged inside.

"Just what do you think you're doing?" Tammy demanded. She was still in her nightgown, but her eyes were narrowed angrily and her hands were balled into fists at her side.

Tessa eyed her warily. "I'm getting ready to take a shower," she replied. "What are you doing up so early?" Usually Tammy didn't surface until noon.

"I wanted to tell you a thing or two," Tammy snarled. "And I didn't want to miss you, so I set the alarm. Just what the heck have you been telling Doreen?''

Tessa stared at her a moment. So Doreen *had* confronted her daughter. She had believed her. ''Tammy, listen, why don't we sit down—''

''I don't need to sit down for what I've got to say to you.'' She began to pace the room.

Tessa decided to try to get her sister to calm down. She didn't want her so upset she wouldn't listen. If this ''intervention'' was going to work, it had to be handled just right. ''Look.'' She tried a tentative smile, but Tammy's belligerent expression didn't change. ''I know you think I've probably run around behind your back to get you in trouble.''

''That's exactly what you've done. You went running to Doreen to tell her that I drink.'' Tammy glared at her sister.

Tessa took a deep breath. This wasn't going to be easy. Too bad she hadn't had time to get to the library and read up on the subject. ''I know it looks bad, but you've got to listen to me. You're right, I did talk to Doreen, but I wasn't—''

''So you admit it,'' Tammy interrupted angrily. ''You admit you went and snitched behind my back.''

''I didn't snitch,'' Tessa protested. ''I told her I was worried about how much you drink.''

''My drinking isn't any of your business.''

''How can you say that? We're sisters. Of course it's my business.''

''What a crock,'' Tammy scoffed. ''You didn't even know I existed until a few weeks ago, so let's cut the bull about you being so concerned about me.''

''It's not bull.'' Tessa's own temper began to flare. ''I do care about you, and believe me, talking to your mother isn't exactly my idea of fun. But I did it because I'm worried about you. You need help.''

''You mean you did it for my own good,'' Tammy said sarcastically. ''That's always a good one. That used to be Doreen's favorite line when I was a kid. But I didn't believe her then and I don't believe you now. Nobody cares about me. No one ever has and no one ever will.''

Tessa clenched her hands into fists. This wasn't going at all well. On television, when you stuck your nose into someone else's life, they were usually maudlin and grateful. Tammy was just plain pissed. But Tessa wasn't going to give up. Angry or not, she was going to make her sister listen to her. ''You don't mean what you're saying,'' she said, fighting to keep her own voice calm and reasonable. ''You have to know I care about you. And in her own way, so does Doreen. Look, you're upset.''

''Damned right I'm upset,'' Tammy snapped. She started pacing back and forth in front of the bed. ''Who wouldn't be when their own sister snuck around behind their back and told a pack of lies about them. God, after all I've done for you. You come into my house and start telling lies about me.''

''Lies!'' Tessa gaped at her. Did Tammy really

believe she didn't have a drinking problem? But that was impossible. No one could be that stupid. "I didn't tell any lies and you know it."

"Oh, didn't you?" Tammy smiled nastily. "All I know is that you tried to get me in trouble. And we both know why you did it, don't we? So let's cut the crap that you're doing it for my own good."

"Tammy . . ." Tessa was going to control her temper even if it killed her. "You're not being fair. I talked to your mother because I'm worried about you. Alex is worried about you. Anyone with two eyes in their head can see what you're doing to yourself."

"Let's get something straight." Tammy stopped right in front of Tessa. "What I'm doing to myself is none of your business. Got it? If I want to take a drink occasionally, I will. I don't need you or anyone else telling me how to run my life. You understand? And let's leave Alex out of this. This is between you and me."

"That's the stupidest thing I ever heard," Tessa sputtered, ignoring the crack about Alex. "You don't 'occasionally take a drink,' you're sauced all the time. Do you really think it's normal for a seventeen-year-old girl to spend practically every waking moment holed up in her room?"

"Stop pretending you're concerned with my welfare," Tammy shot back. "We both know why you ran snitching to Doreen."

Tessa had had it. "Oh yeah. Why?"

Tammy gave her a long, direct stare. "You did it because you want me grounded," she said slowly, maliciously. "You did it because you're jealous."

"Jealous!" Tessa couldn't believe her ears. It was one thing for Doreen to accuse her of being jealous, but having Tammy say the same thing just was the last straw. "Of what?"

"Of everything." Tammy sauntered over to the bed and sat down. "My clothes, my car, my friends, and my money. Did you think I hadn't noticed how much you like my things? God, it's harder to keep you out of my closet than it is to keep a two-year-old away from ice cream."

Tessa's eyes filled with angry tears. This was so unfair. "But you offered to let me wear your clothes."

"Yeah, because I felt sorry for anyone having to walk around in those tacky rags you have."

Hurt speared through her like a knife, but she fought it and the anger back. She was going to be mature about this no matter how many nasty things her sister said to her. Tammy couldn't possibly mean what she was saying. She couldn't. "And you offered to let me drive your car."

"Only because you don't have one and I took pity on you." Tammy gave her another cold smile. "So let's get something straight. If you ever go running to Doreen again, I'll have you packed up and on the next plane out of here. Got it? The party'll be over for you."

Tessa stared at her, so surprised by the streak of maliciousness in her sister she literally couldn't speak.

"No more wearing Tammy's pretty outfits, no more driving around in a convertible, no more having fun in the sun with Tammy's friends." She got up, stalked to the door, and jerked it open. "I'm the one that had you brought here," she said coldly, "and I can get rid of you just as quickly. Remember that." With that, she walked out and slammed the door.

Shocked, Tessa stood and stared dumbly at the closed door for a good minute. Finally, she stumbled toward the unmade bed and flopped down on it. She didn't know whether to use her fists on the pillow or pull the covers over her head and have a good cry.

Anger and hurt battled to take over her emotions. She was angry at Tammy for saying those stupid things, but a part of her was really, really hurt, too. How could Tammy think she was such a lowlife that she'd try to get her grounded out of jealousy? She wasn't in the least jealous of her sister; in fact, after a firsthand look at her birth mother, Tessa was glad she'd been adopted. Maybe her folks weren't rich and maybe they couldn't give her fancy clothes and a car, but by golly, they cared enough to make sure she didn't drink herself to death.

By midafternoon, Tessa had calmed down. Tammy was still closeted in her room and Doreen was out at a Save the Whales committee meeting. Tessa wandered into the kitchen and stared at the refrigerator. She wasn't hungry, but she knew she ought to eat something. That little scene with her sister had ruined her appetite. She was just reaching for the door handle when the phone on the kitchen wall rang.

As Tammy had her own private line and couldn't be bothered to pick up one of the extensions upstairs, Tessa reached for the receiver. "Hello."

"Hi, it's me." Alex's voice was annoyingly cheerful. "How did it go?"

"Lousy," Tessa replied. She knew he was talking about the alleged intervention. She turned and stared at the door. It would be just her luck for Tammy to sneak in and catch Tessa talking about her. "She wouldn't listen to a thing I said. What's worse, Doreen had told her that I'd talked to her."

"Guess she was kinda mad, huh?"

"She went ballistic."

Alex sighed. "I hope that doesn't mean you're giving up."

Tessa wasn't sure if she was giving up or not. The things that Tammy had said to her had really hurt. How could you help someone who hated you? "I don't know," she finally said. "I don't think Tammy is going to take kindly to my interfering in her life."

"Interfering? Don't be silly, you're her sister," Alex said. "You're not interfering, you're trying to help her."

"Yeah, but she doesn't see it that way." Tessa sighed. "The truth is, Tammy was so ticked at me, she wouldn't let me get a word in edgewise. There was no real intervention, even if I knew how in the heck to do one; I didn't have the chance. She was too busy yelling at me to hear a word I said."

"Hey," Alex said softly, hearing the misery in Tessa's voice, "you did your best."

"Best doesn't count when someone thinks you're only trying to get them in trouble. Tammy thinks I'm jealous of her. She says that I was just trying to get her grounded."

Alex said nothing for a moment. "You're upset, aren't you?"

"A little. It wasn't exactly fun, you know."

"I know. Why don't I come by and pick you up," he suggested. "I'm through working for the day. We'll drive over to the beach and grab a bite to eat. We've got to talk about this. You can tell me everything that happened."

Tessa hesitated. She had to remember that Alex was Tammy's boyfriend, not hers. "I don't know," she muttered. "If Tammy finds out, she might get mad."

"Tammy's probably passed out by now," Alex shot back. "And who the heck cares if she gets mad? From what you've told me, she ought to be worried about you being mad at her. She has a lousy mouth sometimes."

"No kidding." Tessa made up her mind. She wasn't jealous of her sister and she wasn't going to back off just because Tammy told her to. Her sister needed help. "Okay, I'll be out front."

Alex arrived ten minutes later. Tessa yanked open the door and jumped in the front seat before he even came to a stop. "Let's get going," she said. "I don't want her to see us together."

He raised his eyebrows but said nothing as he pulled back out onto the street. Tessa felt her cheeks turning red. God, this was so embarrassing. She'd made it sound like they were sneaking off on a date or something.

"I mean, she's already paranoid," Tessa explained hastily. "I don't want her to see us going off together and having her think we're up to something."

"But we are up to something." Alex shrugged his shoulders. "We're trying to save her life."

"Yes, but she doesn't know that. And after what I've been through in the past twenty-four hours, I'd just as soon not have her coming after me with an ice pick because she thinks I'm trying to steal her boyfriend."

He laughed. "You watch too many movies. All right, I get your point." He slanted her a speculative glance. "But she wouldn't, you know."

"Wouldn't what?" Tessa asked.

"Come after you with an ice pick. She'd be more likely to go on a bender."

"Right." Tessa sighed. "And that's why we're here. We've got to figure out a way to keep her sober."

For the rest of the ride to the beach, they didn't talk much. Both of them were thinking. When they got to the coast, Alex pulled into a parking lot. "Keep your eyes open for a space," he instructed.

"There's one." Tessa pointed straight ahead to a spot that had just been vacated by a minivan. He drove in and parked. They got out and, without speaking, headed for the sand. If Tessa hadn't been so preoccupied with worrying about Tammy, she'd have enjoyed the bright sunshine and clean, crisp breeze coming off the Pacific.

"So what do we do now?" she asked as they started walking on the hard-packed sand next to the water's edge.

"I've been thinking about that," he replied. He stared out at the ocean. "Maybe we should try another intervention."

"What good would that do?" Tessa shrugged. "She wouldn't listen. Tammy refuses to believe she has a problem."

"Maybe she'll take it more seriously if I'm there, too," he suggested. "One thing I do know, Tammy does respect me."

Tessa slanted him a quick glance and then stumbled to one side as Alex jerked her back to avoid an incoming wave that had come farther up on the sand than the previous ones. "Thanks," she mumbled. "I don't know, Alex. No matter how much she respects you, I still don't think it will work. Besides, neither of us really knows how to do this intervention thing. I think it takes more than just sitting someone down and telling them they've got a problem."

They'd come to an outcrop of rocks at the edge of the low bluff. Alex headed toward them. "Let's sit down; I've been on my feet all morning." He found a flat spot and sat down, scooting to one side to make room for Tessa. She plopped down next to him.

"Okay," he mused, "you're right. We don't know how to do an intervention. But what other choice do we have? We've got to do something."

His arm brushed Tessa's, and for a moment she simply enjoyed the feel of his skin nudging her bare arm. She was wearing a scoop-necked, short-sleeve, red T-shirt and jeans, and she wished she'd worn something nicer. The way her luck had been running lately, she might not have too many more chances to see Alex. As soon as the thought entered her head, she felt guilty. She was supposed to be thinking of ways to help her sister, not about Alex.

"I know," she agreed. "But what? I think those intervention things only work if there's a professional of some kind involved. You know, like a social worker or a psychologist."

"Or Tammy's parents." Alex shook his head in disgust. "God, I don't believe her mother. How can she be so dumb? Does she honestly think it's normal for her seventeen-year-old daughter to hole up in that bedroom all day? What does she think she's doing in there, writing her memoirs?"

"Doreen doesn't want to believe it," Tessa replied. "But to give her credit, she did confront Tammy about it."

"Come on," he snorted in derision. "She probably stuck her head into Tammy's room for ten seconds and asked if she'd been nipping at the dinner wine. Geez, I'm amazed she even bothered to do that. Guess Doreen's finally trying to go for the 'mother of the year' award." He broke off suddenly and glanced at Tessa, his expression sheepish. "Sorry, I forgot for a moment she's your mother, too."

"Don't apologize," Tessa said. "I feel pretty much the same way. Besides, she's not really my mom; she only gave birth to me. If my real mom was here and it was me drinking and not Tammy, I'd be in rehab so fast it would make your head spin."

They sat in companionable silence for a few moments. Tessa watched a couple of seagulls circle over the rocks, their cries echoing in the quiet afternoon. Finally, she said, "I don't know what we're going to do. For God's sake, we're only kids. We can't handle a problem like this. We don't know what we're doing, we don't know how to get Tammy to wake up to the fact that she's an alcoholic, and I, for one, am getting a little ticked off that we have to! Why should *we* deal with this?" she asked, suddenly so angry she couldn't sit still.

She jumped to her feet and faced the ocean, her hands clenched tightly at her side. The past two days had taken a toll on her emotions. Suddenly the awful confrontations came back to her in a horrible, overwhelming rush. Doreen's cold anger. Tammy's hateful, malicious words. Both of them had accused her of jealousy. What really frightened Tessa was that there'd been a small grain of truth in the charge. One teeny, tiny part of her had been jealous of Tammy. But not for any of the reasons they'd said. She hadn't cared about Tammy's clothes or car or house. Somewhere deep inside her, she'd been jealous of something entirely different.

Tammy hadn't been given away.

"Hey," Alex said, touching her arm gently. "Lighten up."

"Lighten up!" Tessa whirled around to glare at him. "That's okay for you to say. You're not living in that house. You didn't have to face Doreen or Tammy."

"No," Alex agreed softly. "I didn't have to face them, but I would have if you hadn't. You took a big chance, Tessa, and that says a lot about what you are. The fact that even though both Doreen and Tammy raked you over the coals, you're still willing to try and help says a lot."

She bit her lip and looked down at the sand. Heck, just when she was working up a good case of really righteous anger, he goes and says something like that. "I'm not so special," she mumbled.

He reached over and took her hand. "Yes, you are."

As suddenly as it had come, the anger went out of her. Maybe it was because now that she'd faced the truth, now that she acknowledged and understood that part of her that had been jealous of Tammy, she could let it go.

Or maybe it was because Alex thought she was a saint. She didn't know, and right now, with him holding her hand and gazing at her with that expression on his face, she didn't much care.

They remained that way for a few moments, a quiet, unspoken acknowledgment of their feelings for each other. Feelings they couldn't afford to deal with now. Finally, Alex tugged Tessa back down beside him. "So what do we do now?" he asked.

"Beats me. But before we brainstorm our next step, there's something else I'd like to ask you."

"Ask away." He grinned impishly. "Keep in mind, though, I don't answer embarrassing questions."

She laughed and then her expression turned serious. "Tammy said something really weird to me today."

"Tammy says lots of weird things," he replied, "especially when she's mad."

"But this was different. She said she was the one that had me brought here." Tessa had deliberately pushed this to the back of her mind. The idea that it hadn't been her birth mother, but her sister who'd wanted to see her, had hurt. But she wanted to face it now, just like she was forcing herself to face a lot of hard truths. "Do you think she was lying?"

Alex dropped his gaze and stared at the tip of his shoe. "I don't know." He looked up at her, his expression guarded. "Why? Is it important to you who wanted you to come? I mean, isn't the main thing that you're here?"

Tessa shrugged. She didn't want to admit, even to herself, how important it was. But darn it, why couldn't it have been Doreen who'd wanted to meet her? Maybe the woman wasn't exactly a poster picture for Mother's Day, but you'd think she'd have some curiosity about how the daughter she'd given away had turned out. "Yeah," Tessa lied. "The main thing is, I'm here. It doesn't matter which one of them wanted me to come."

Alex didn't say anything for a moment; he simply looked at her. "You sure?"

"Yeah, I'm sure." She blinked against a sudden gust of wind and told herself it really didn't matter who'd wanted her to come to Lansdale. But the wetness filling her eyes wasn't just a reaction to the strong, salty breezes. "Anyway, we've got more important things to worry about now."

"Like what we're going to do about Tammy," Alex agreed glumly.

"Maybe we could get some of the other kids to help," Tessa suggested.

"Nah." Alex shook his head. "First of all, they're too much in awe of Tammy to believe the truth, and secondly, half of them drink themselves." He kicked at the sand. "It's just us, kiddo. You and me. If we don't do something, no one will."

"But why is it our responsibility?" Tessa cried, overwhelmed by the enormity of what they faced. "We're just kids. This isn't fair."

"Tell me about it," Alex agreed. "But what choice do we have?"

Tessa knew they didn't have any choice at all. Doreen and Tammy both refused to face the truth. Harold was too busy playing golf. Alex was right. They were the only ones who could help Tammy. "But what if we screw it up? What if we fail? What if our attempts to make Tammy get help backfire and she starts drinking even more?"

"It's a chance we've got to take," he replied. "Besides, if we don't even try, she'll only get worse. If Tammy keeps on drinking, she'll end up either choking to death on her own vomit or wrapping her car around a tree and killing herself. Can you live with that?"

"Thanks for those graphic images," Tessa said as she repressed a shudder. "So where do we go from here?"

"Hey, I've got it," he said excitedly. "Maybe we could talk to Harold Mercer."

"No way." Tessa shook her head.

"Why not?"

"Two reasons." She held out a finger. "First, he wouldn't believe us, and second"—she held out another finger—"he'd go right to Doreen."

"But isn't that what we want him to do," Alex pressed, "go to Doreen? Make her open her eyes to the fact that her kid's drinking herself to death."

"All it will do is tick both of them off," Tessa said firmly. "Then they'll have me on the first bus, plane, train, or cattle car out of here. Even if you're the one that tries to talk to Harold, I'm the one they'll blame."

"We don't know that for sure."

But Tessa did know it. "You weren't the one on the receiving end of Tammy's threats. For that matter, Doreen dropped a few hints along those lines, too. Is that what you want, Alex? For me to leave? Because that's exactly what'll happen."

Alex stood up. He put his hands on Tessa's shoulders and drew her close. She nestled into him, drawing strength from his warmth. "No," he said softly, his mouth muffled against her hair, "that's the last thing I want. I can't even stand the idea that come September you're going back home."

Tessa shut her eyes against the flash of guilt that swept over her. Why now? Why, out of all the guys she'd ever met, did she have to start falling for the one boy she couldn't have? Alex was Tammy's boyfriend; she had to remember that. Slowly, reluctantly, she drew away. "But I do have to leave. And we both know it."

"But not yet," he said firmly.

"No," she agreed, "not yet."

Hand in hand, they started walking back up the beach toward the parking lot. Despite their problems, Tessa couldn't help but smile at the beauty of the day. A group of children, screaming with laughter, scampered in and out of the water as she and Alex walked past. Overhead, the seagulls added their loud cries to the sound of the kids playing in the surf. The sun shone brightly against the waves, turning spray into cascading diamond streamers of water and the sky was a brilliant blue. For a moment, for just a brief moment, she told herself that she'd forget she was with a boy she had no right to be with and that her sister was an alcoholic.

But all too quickly, reality raised its ugly head. As they reached the edge of the parking lot, Alex suddenly stopped. "I've got it."

"What?"

"I've figured out a way to do this. A way to

force Tammy and the Mercers to face the fact that she drinks. God, have we been dumb. The answers have been right in front of us all along. I can't believe we didn't see it."

"What are you talking about?"

"What if Harold and Doreen actually see how much Tammy drinks?" Alex asked. "What if they see that she's stealing their booze right and left and that she gets so plastered when she goes out that she can't even drive?"

"And exactly how do we make them do that?" Tessa asked. "You told me that Tammy's been drinking for years, but neither of them has noticed."

Alex grinned triumphantly. "But that's because they didn't have to. But what if they did? What if they couldn't keep avoiding the issue anymore?"

"And precisely how do we accomplish that?"

"We make Tammy face the consequences of her actions," Alex explained. "That ought to wake the Mercers up pretty quickly. From now on, there'll be no more driving Tammy home because she's so blitzed she can't find her car, no more telling people she's up in her room nursing a migraine when in reality, she's dead drunk, and no more putting her to bed when she's too loaded to get there under her own steam. In other words, Tessa, from now on, little Tammy is on her own. If she wants to drink, then she faces the music. To put it simply, we stop covering for her."

CHAPTER
EIGHT

Dear Diary,

Today we start the new plan. I sure hope it works. I've got a feeling this is our last crack at it. If refusing to cover for my dear sister doesn't get Doreen and Harold out of their coma, nothing will.

But Alex said something that really bothered me when we were driving home yesterday. It was about how we'd both covered for Tammy. "I'm as guilty of it as you are," he said. "I've been doing it for a long time. But when you came along, she didn't need me anymore—she had you to do the dirty work."

I know I shouldn't brood over it, but I can't help but think that maybe the reason that Tammy wanted me to come here was because she sensed that Alex was getting fed up and she needed someone else.

Tessa read the words she'd just written and tried to ignore the sharp stab of pain they brought. Could it possibly be true? Had her sister only wanted to meet her, to spend the summer with her, just so she'd have someone to run interference? Was Tammy that manipulative? Had she brought her here only because she wanted someone to do the driving, tell the lies, and distract Doreen and Harold from the real problem? Tessa didn't want to think it was true, but now that the thought had crept into her head, she couldn't make it go away.

She put her diary in the drawer, got up, and went downstairs. Doreen was sitting at the kitchen table, a cup of coffee in front of her. "Good morning," she said formally.

"Morning," Tessa replied. She noticed that Doreen didn't crack a smile.

Doreen put her cup down. "What are your plans for today?"

"I don't know," Tessa said as she poured herself a cup of coffee. "Just hang out, I guess."

"Tammy said you were going to a party tonight." Doreen got up and smoothed a nonexistent wrinkle out of her peacock-blue skirt. "That's nice. I like to see you girls having a good time together. Harold and I are going to a dinner party at the Raymonds'."

An idea began to form in Tessa's mind. "Uh, what time do you think you'll be back?"

"I don't really know." Doreen frowned slightly. "I suppose around ten or ten-thirty. Why?"

"Just curious." Tessa gave her a brilliant smile.

"Are you going to be busy today? I thought maybe you and Tammy and I could go shopping or something?"

Doreen gave her a quick, surprised smile and then started for the door. "I'm sorry, I wish I could. But I'm going to be tied up all day. We're making the final plans for the Friends of the Library luncheon and then I've got to go to a committee meeting for the art museum. But maybe we can do it one day next week," she called over her shoulder as she stepped into the hallway. "I'll check my Day-Timer."

"Yeah, sure," Tessa muttered. It wasn't part of the plan, but for a few moments there, she'd thought that maybe if she could get Doreen to actually spend some time with Tammy, she might see for herself that the girl had a problem.

Tessa didn't see much of Tammy for the rest of the day. As usual, she spent most of it in her room. Tessa read for a while, tidied up her own room, wrote a letter to her parents, and wished that Alex would call. But he was working a day shift so that he could go to Todd Huckstadter's party that night.

She spotted her sister once in passing as she was going down the hall late in the afternoon. But Tammy only gave her a cold smile and continued walking. Tessa noticed, though, that she couldn't smell any alcohol on her sister.

At seven o'clock, Tessa started to get ready for the party. This time she went to her own closet and pulled out a simple emerald-green-and-white scoop-necked cotton dress. A few minutes later she stood in front of the mirror. Tessa grinned at her reflection. The rounded neck showed off the line of her throat and the fitted waist emphasized her slim figure. She thought that she looked pretty darned good. Her clothes could never compete with her sister's, but she didn't care about that anymore. From now on, she'd wear her own things. They might not be as expensive or as elegant as Tammy's, but they were hers.

"Well, admiring ourself, are we?" Tammy said.

Tessa whirled around and saw her standing in the bedroom door. "As a matter of fact, I was. I'd forgotten how much I liked this outfit. Mom and I found it at a swap meet. Your dress is really pretty, too."

"It's okay." Tammy glanced down at the pale pink slip dress she wore and shrugged. "I just yanked the first thing I could find out of the closet, but it'll do for Todd's party."

Her dress was a designer original that had cost at least a couple of hundred bucks and they both knew it. Tessa smiled warmly, determined not to feel like Cinderella going to her first ball. "I think we'll be the two prettiest girls at the party. Maybe we should get going; it's a good hike over to Todd's."

"Hike?" Tammy repeated the word like she'd never heard it before. "What are you talking about? We'll drive."

Tessa had been waiting for this. "Well, if we drive, you won't be able to drink."

Tammy's eyes narrowed suspiciously. "Why not? You'll be the one driving home, not me."

" 'Fraid not." Tessa shrugged nonchalantly. "You see, after that little talk we had, I've decided I'm not driving your car anymore. Or wearing your clothes."

"But you'll hang out with my friends." Tammy sneered. "Seems to me, if you're going to play the martyr, you should go all the way."

"But they're my friends now, too." Tessa replied. "Todd called me himself to ask me to come." That much was true at least. Though Tessa didn't add that Todd had really called to talk to Tammy and he'd only invited Tessa because she happened to answer the phone.

Tammy glared at her. "I know what you're trying to do."

"And what's that?"

"Make me feel bad because I lost my temper the other day." She whirled around and stomped toward the door. "It's not going to work and I'm not walking with you to that damned party." She slammed the door on her way out.

Tammy didn't walk to the party either. As Tessa was trudging up the hill toward Todd's house, she saw Jeremy's car go past. Tammy was sitting in the front seat with him.

The party would have been fun, but Tessa was too busy keeping an eye on Tammy to enjoy it. By the time Alex showed up at eight-thirty, she was beginning to think they'd made a serious mistake. Her sister was drinking more than ever.

"How's it going?" Alex asked as he sat down on the sofa next to her.

"Not too good. She's out in the backyard with Jack Driscoll and Patrick Rand," Tessa said. She stole a quick look at him and her heart rate jumped into double time. He wore a pair of faded jeans and a fitted short-sleeve white shirt that fit snugly across his chest. He looked incredibly handsome.

"The serious drinkers," Alex muttered in disgust. "But I thought you refused to drive tonight? How's she planning on getting home?"

"I didn't drive," Tessa snapped, a little annoyed at the accusing tone in his voice. "I walked. *She* got a ride with Jeremy."

"Hey, I wasn't taking a shot at you." Alex glanced at her in surprise. "I was just asking, okay?"

"Sorry I snapped," she said, giving him a quick smile. "I guess I'm nervous. If this doesn't work, I don't know what we'll do."

"It'll work," he said confidently. "I'm going to cut out early so she can't bum a ride with me." He rose to his feet. "I think I'll have a talk with Jeremy, make sure he doesn't come to her rescue."

Tessa stared at him in dismay. She'd hoped that he would offer to take *her* home. She didn't particularly want to walk home alone at night.

"Don't worry," he said, correctly reading the expression on her face. "I was going to have you come with me. If neither of us is here, then she has to make her own way home."

Tessa smiled in relief. Then her expression so-

bered. "I don't know if that's such a good idea,"
she said. "I mean, what if she bums a ride with
Jack or Patrick? I don't trust either of those guys."

"Neither do I," Alex replied. "But if we're going to stop covering for her, we stop covering for
her and let her take the consequences."

"But that could be dangerous," Tessa warned.
"Really dangerous. I thought the whole idea here
was to keep her from killing herself. If she gets
into a car with either of those two jerks, she still
might end up going through a windshield."

"It's a chance we have to take," Alex said. "I
don't like it any more than you do, but we're not
doing her any good if we hang around playing
nursemaid."

Tessa gave up arguing. Alex was right. She just
had to trust that whatever angel looked out for
drunks and idiots would keep a really good eye on
her sister.

Shortly after ten o'clock, Alex told Tammy he
was leaving, and giving Tessa a ride home.
Tammy's only response was to wave her wineglass
at him and smile. Tessa, with one last worried
glance at her sister, followed Alex out to the car.
As she climbed into the front seat she sent up a
short silent prayer that Tammy would get home in
one piece.

Tessa and Alex didn't talk on the short drive to
the Mercer house. They were both too worried
about Tammy. Pulling up to the curb, Alex cut the
engine. "What time are the Mercers supposed to
be home?"

"Doreen said around ten or ten-thirty. They're at a dinner party tonight." Tessa glanced at her watch. "They'll probably be here anytime now."

"If we're really lucky, they might pull up just as Tammy is getting home." Alex chuckled. "As we were leaving I saw one of the neighbors looking out their front window. The cops ought to be breaking it up pretty soon."

"I hope so," Tessa murmured. In the quiet car, she could feel her heart pounding against her chest. She ought to be thinking about Tammy, but sitting here with Alex, all she could concentrate on was him. And she had no right to feel this way. Tessa stiffened her spine and reached for the door handle. "I'd better get inside."

"Don't go," Alex said quickly. He reached over and put his hand on her arm. "Uh, we haven't had a chance to talk or anything. Besides, it's still early."

But Tessa knew that sitting in this dark, intimate car with her sister's boyfriend was too dangerous. She really liked Alex. Liked him more than any boy she'd ever met. And she couldn't have him. "Alex," she began, "I don't think this is a good idea. . . ."

"I know, I know." He waved his hand impatiently. "I'm Tammy's boyfriend and you've got a case of the guilts, right?"

"Right."

"But it doesn't have to be that way," he said softly. "I mean, things could change. . . ."

She leaned over and laid her fingers across his

mouth, stopping him in midsentence. "The only change we can worry about right now is getting Tammy to admit she's got a problem. Getting her into some kind of rehab program. Anything else will have to wait."

He stared at her for a long moment, then gently reached up, wrapped his fingers around hers, and kissed the tips. "You're right," he murmured. "But when we get this problem taken care of, you and I are going to have a long talk."

Tessa smiled wanly and got out of the car. Alex didn't pull away from the curb until she was safely inside the house. Then she settled down behind the curtains to wait for her sister.

But once again, Tammy outfoxed them. Within half an hour a cab pulled up, and Tammy, stumbling only a little, got out.

"Damn," Tessa muttered as she hurried up the stairs and into her bedroom, "She called a cab. Who'd have thought she'd pull the oldest drunk's trick in the book."

Despite Doreen's protests that she didn't believe her daughter had a drinking problem, Tessa found her in the wine cupboard counting the bottles one morning. Doreen flushed slightly when she realized Tessa was there, but said nothing. She just hurried out to whatever committee meeting awaited her. Apparently, Tammy must have figured that Doreen was onto her, too, because in the days that followed, she stopped stealing her parents' booze.

But she didn't stop drinking.

Tessa had no idea where she was getting her supply, but someone was buying it for her. Furthermore, she'd wised up. She no longer holed up in her room all the time. Now she went out for "walks," and when she came back, her eyes might be slightly glassy, but she didn't stumble and her breath was as minty fresh as a mouthwash commercial. Tessa wondered where she went, but she couldn't quite bring herself to follow Tammy. There was something really ugly about actually spying on her sister.

Tammy often went out at night, too. But she never drove. She generally conned Jeremy or Joleen into giving her a ride, and now she didn't bother to invite Tessa to go along with her. As a matter of fact, she pretty much ignored Tessa these days, despite Tessa's attempts to stay close. All in all, it was pretty depressing. All in all, it was driving Tessa out of her mind.

To top it off, Tessa hadn't heard from her own parents in over a week. She was beginning to think she'd become invisible. Tammy ignored her, Harold and Doreen treated her with the distant politeness one shows an acquaintance, Alex was working long hours at the video store, and her own mom and dad couldn't be bothered to write a darned letter or pick up the phone.

Finally, one afternoon Tessa realized that she'd had it. She stomped down the stairs and glared at the silent, empty living room. No one was here. Tammy was out, probably meeting her connection, she thought angrily as she stalked to the phone and snatched it up. She dialed Alex's number at the video store. He answered. "Alex," she began, "we've got to talk. This isn't working."

"I know," he admitted glumly. "She's got the other kids wrapped around her finger. I tried to tell Jeremy and Joleen they weren't helping, but they haven't got half a brain between them, so I couldn't even get them to listen."

"When do you get off work?"

"In ten minutes," he replied. "I'm coming over. Is Tammy there?"

"No," Tessa answered. "Why?"

"Because there's something else we've got to talk about."

Tessa bit her lip. She didn't like the sound of that. If Alex backed off now, she'd have to handle her sister all by herself. And she couldn't do it, she just couldn't do it. She was only seventeen, for God's sake. "Uh, look, Alex—"

"I've got to go now, my boss just walkcd in," he said quickly. "We'll talk when I get there."

Tessa paced the house for a good twenty minutes before she heard Alex's car pull up. She met him at the front door. "Look," she began as he came in, "I know that Tammy's a real pain in the butt, but you can't quit on me now."

"I don't intend to," he said brusquely. He reached for her hand. "Let's go out by the pool. I've been cooped up behind a counter all day and I need some fresh air."

Confused, she followed him outside. "I'll leave this door open," she said as she stepped onto the patio. "I'm hoping my parents will call."

"Okay," he murmured absently as he sat down at the table.

Tessa took the seat opposite him, shifting slightly to find a comfortable position on the heavy iron seat. "I can't stand the suspense," she announced. "What's up? Have you got another idea about how we can get Tammy into rehab?"

"This isn't about Tammy," he said, turning his head and staring at the still water of the swimming pool. "Well, it is, but only kinda indirectly."

"Huh?"

He drew a deep breath. "I've decided to break up with Tammy."

"What?" Tessa was dumbfounded. "Are you nuts? You can't break up with her, she'll go ballistic."

He turned his head and looked at her. "Don't you want me to? Don't you want to be with me? I thought we had something going between us, something really good. I thought you felt the same way. I thought you liked me."

"I do," Tessa cried. "But I thought we'd decided to put those feelings away until we got this mess with Tammy sorted out."

He shook his head. "We'll never get it taken care of," he said bluntly. "Only Tammy can do that. I've done a lot of thinking about this and one of the reasons I haven't been around too much is because I went to the library and did a little reading on alcoholism. The bottom line is that Tammy's the one that has to decide she wants to quit. We can't do it for her.''

''But—''

He waved his hand impatiently. ''There's no buts about it. Until she figures out she's got a problem, until she decides she doesn't want to live her life in a bottle, there's nothing we can do.''

''So we give up?'' Tessa demanded. ''Just like that, we back off and let her kill herself?'' She'd done some thinking, too. The awful thing was, her mind had come to the same conclusion he had, but her heart just wouldn't let her give up on her sister without a fight.

''We've done everything we can,'' he persisted. ''What's left to do? The Mercers are useless. They've got their heads buried so deep in the sand it would take a bulldozer to dig them out. Tammy doesn't think she has a problem, and even worse, she's gotten really good at conning everyone else into helping her. So you tell me, what the hell do we do now? Keep sneaking around her back so we can see each other?''

''We haven't been doing that,'' she protested.

''Oh yes, we have,'' he shot back. ''To be perfectly honest, that's the only reason I've tried this hard with Tammy. It was a good excuse to be with you.''

''But I thought you cared about her?''

''I did—I mean, I do. But I care about you more and I'm tired of feeling guilty about it.'' He laughed harshly. ''Tammy's treated me like dirt and I took it because I thought she needed me. But she doesn't; she doesn't need anyone. Look at the way she's turned on you."

Tessa couldn't deny what he said. It was true. Tammy hadn't bothered with her since she'd stopped covering for her drinking. No more little chats in Tammy's bedroom at night, no more shopping trips to the mall, no more nothing, not even a polite hello every once in a while. "Okay," she said softly. "I can't deny what you're saying. Tammy hasn't been very nice to me lately. But she's my sister, and whether she cares about me or not, I care about her."

"Do you care about me?"

Tessa nodded. "More than I've ever cared before. But I've got a feeling that if you break up with Tammy, things will blow up."

"You mean she might send you packing?"

"Yeah. Like you said, she's made it pretty clear she doesn't need me anymore. I think she only keeps me around because she doesn't want Harold or Doreen asking any questions. But if you break up with her, she can go running to them crying that I've stolen her boyfriend and I'll be out of here in two seconds flat."

"But Doreen's your mother, too," Alex insisted. "I don't care what Tammy said, Doreen must have wanted you here this summer, too."

Tessa wished it were true, but in her heart, she knew it wasn't. "I've gotten closer to Mr. Lockhart, the gardener, than I have to Doreen. For God's sake, I've barely seen the woman this summer. She doesn't even know me. All she wants is a peaceful life so she can have her committee meetings and charity lunches,'' Tessa said honestly. "She wouldn't have any problems packing my bags and kicking me out of here.''

"All right, all right,'' Alex said impatiently. "Even if the worst happens and they send you packing, is that such a bad thing?''

"Is that what you want?'' Tessa asked.

"Of course not,'' he insisted. "But maybe it wouldn't be so bad. Los Angeles isn't that far away. I've got a car, you know. I could come see you on weekends. Besides, in September I'll be down there anyway. I'm going to UCLA, remember? Heck, Tessa, anything's better than what we're doing now. It's driving me crazy.''

It was driving her crazy, too. Tessa thought about what he'd said. Maybe he was right. Not just about them, but about everything. It wasn't as if she was doing Tammy much good. You couldn't help someone who wasn't even speaking to you.

"Well, well, well.'' Tammy's voice came from the open patio door. "What do we have here?''

Tessa could feel her cheeks flame. She had no reason to feel guilty, but she did anyway. "Hi, Tammy.''

"We were just talking about you,'' Alex said. He glanced at Tessa. "Uh, why don't you leave us alone for a few minutes?''

Tessa was already on her feet and heading for the house. This was one conversation she didn't want any part of. "Okay, I'll see you later.'' She brushed past her sister and went inside.

Entering the kitchen, she opened the fridge and searched for a soft drink. She wasn't thirsty, but it gave her something to do.

Then she heard Tammy scream. Tessa couldn't stand it. She flew back toward the patio and came to a skidding halt by the door. Tammy was pacing furiously, her eyes flashing with rage at Alex.

"You've just been using me," she screamed at him. "All this time, you've just been using me."

"Tammy, that's not true," Alex said.

"Don't give me that crap," she cried bitterly. "That's why you called me an alcoholic, that's why you keep telling me I had a problem, so you'd have an excuse to dump me."

"I don't need an excuse," he yelled back at her. "I can't handle you anymore, Tammy. You need help and you need some lessons in how to treat people."

"From you?" She laughed bitterly. "Oh yeah, you're a real role model, aren't you? You've spent half the summer trying to convince me I'm sick so you can sneak around with my tramp of a sister—"

"Leave Tessa out of this."

"Like hell I will," Tammy snapped. "We were getting along just fine until she came along. She's ruined everything. She's tried to take everything away from me, but she's not taking you!"

"She didn't take me away," he said, "the booze did. Having a drink was always more important to you than I was, and we both know it."

"That's not true."

"Where were you when I won the city championship in track?'' he persisted. ''Where were you when my dad had that heart attack last summer and I really needed someone to help me hang on? Where were you when old man Macomber was going to dump me from senior honors because I let you copy my test? I had to crawl to stay in that class and you didn't lift a finger to help. You just kept pouring the wine down your throat and expected me to clean up the mess.'' He shook his head in disgust. ''I'm through with cleaning up after you, Tammy, and I'm through with you.''

Tammy screamed again, so loudly that Tessa stepped back. Even Alex, now that his anger was spent, looked alarmed.

Tears rolled down her cheeks and her whole body shook. ''I can't stand this,'' she cried, then ran toward the door and into the house.

''Tammy, wait,'' Alex called.

But she didn't stop, she just whizzed past Tessa and stumbled toward the front door. She slowed down only long enough to grab her car keys.

''Alex, we've got to stop her,'' Tessa called as she took off after her. ''She can't drive, she's been drinking.''

Alex looked confused, as though he didn't know what to do.

''I'll go after her,'' Tessa yelled. She sprinted for the front door.

By the time Tessa made it to the driveway, Tammy was behind the wheel. She sobbed hysterically as she tried to jam the key in the ignition. She didn't see Tessa come running up to the car.

"Tammy, you're in no condition to drive," Tessa began.

"Go away," Tammy yelled. She rammed the key in and gave it a vicious flick. The engine turned over and caught. Tessa knew she couldn't let her sister drive off, so she sprinted around the car and yanked open the passenger door. She managed to fling herself inside just as Tammy slammed the car into gear and hit the gas.

"For God's sake," Tessa yelled as the vehicle careened backward out of the driveway, "stop the car. You're going to kill someone."

"Maybe I'll kill myself," Tammy cried. "No one would care. Nobody cares about me. No one ever has."

"Tammy, that isn't true." Tessa wondered if she could wrestle the steering wheel away from her. The car shot out onto the street like a cannon.

"The hell it isn't." Tammy stomped hard on the gas, jammed the gearshift out of reverse, and they took off down the hill. "No one cares about me, no one. And now you've taken Alex away from me, too."

"Tammy, slow down," Tessa cried. Houses and telephone poles whizzed past as Tammy pressed the accelerator to the floor and took the corner at the bottom of the hill on two wheels.

"For God's sake, do you want to kill us?" Desperate, Tessa lunged for the steering wheel. But Tammy knocked her arm away. The car swerved hard to the right. Tessa screamed as Tammy tried to regain control, but her reflexes were too slow.

Both girls screamed as the car headed straight for a telephone pole.

There was a loud crash as metal met concrete. Then a deathly silence. Tammy, gasping for breath, looked over at her sister, who was slumped over the dashboard. "Tessa, are you all right?"

But Tessa didn't move.

"Tessa, Tessa," Tammy screamed. "Answer me, damn it!"

But Tessa didn't answer. She couldn't. She was unconscious.

CHAPTER NINE

"Are you going to tell?" Tammy whispered to Alex. She shot a quick, frightened glance at the Mercers, who were standing on the far side of the emergency room talking to one of the policemen.

Alex gave her a disgusted look.

Tammy cringed. She was disgusted with herself for even asking him, but she was scared, too. "Don't look at me like that," she begged. "I'm not being selfish here, I'm doing it for Tessa's own good." She faltered at the sight of the anger that flared in his eyes. "She's my sister, you know. I didn't mean to hurt her. If she hadn't grabbed the wheel—"

"You might both be dead," he interrupted. "I saw the way you drove down that hill. Geez, Tammy, you must have been doing eighty. You're lucky both of you didn't go through the windshield. Oh, I forgot, you were wearing your seat belt, weren't you?''

Tammy's eyes filled with tears. She had been wearing a seat belt. Upset as she'd been, it had been a reflex action to strap it on when she'd gotten in the car. Tessa hadn't put hers on. There hadn't been time. ''Oh God, Alex. I'm sorry. I didn't mean for it to happen, honestly. I was just so upset. I didn't know what I was doing.''

''*You* were upset?'' He sneered. ''Now she's unconscious because she was worried you'd hurt yourself.'' He turned his back and started to walk away, then he stopped and turned to face her. ''You can tell your parents whatever you want,'' he said coldly, ''but I don't think it'll do you much good.''

The fear in Tammy's stomach tightened into a hard knot. The accident was her fault, but she was terrified that if this information leaked out, everyone would hate her. She wasn't worried about losing her license or getting grounded or even being arrested. She was scared that everyone, her mother included, would turn their backs on her and leave her alone with her guilt.

''But no one saw that I was the one really driving the car—'' Tammy began, but Alex cut her off.

''Don't be an idiot. Just because I didn't snitch on you doesn't mean you're home free.'' He smiled derisively. ''The cops didn't buy your story for one minute. They know Tessa wasn't driving that car. I overheard them talking. There was blood on the dashboard from where Tessa hit her head. If you'd been in the passenger seat, like you told them, you'd be the one with the gash on your head. In case you haven't noticed, there isn't a scratch on you.''

Tammy bit her lip. Her sister was lying unconscious in a hospital bed and it was all her fault. Everything was her fault. ''Alex,'' she pleaded softly. ''Please don't hate me. I didn't mean for this to happen.''

He glared at her for a moment and then sighed in defeat as he saw the misery etched on her face. ''I know.'' His shoulders slumped. ''I know. You didn't mean to hurt her. You never mean to hurt anyone.''

''I really didn't,'' she said, blinking hard to keep the tears from falling. ''She's my sister. I—I love her, and when she wakes up, she's going to hate me.''

''No, she won't,'' he said softly. Relenting, he walked back and put his arm around her shoulders. ''Tessa doesn't have it in her to hate anyone. Come on, let's go see if we can get any news out of your parents. They must have heard something by now.''

The policeman, after giving Tammy a long, thoughtful inspection, finished talking to Doreen as the two of them approached.

''Is there any news?'' Tammy asked.

''No,'' Doreen replied. Her face was white, her eyes frightened. ''The doctors are still working on her. She hasn't regained consciousness.''

''Has anyone called her parents?'' Alex asked.

He knew how close Tessa was to her folks and also knew that she would want them here.

"Harold's calling them now," Doreen said. She looked at Tammy. "Tell me what happened? And don't give me that nonsense about Tessa driving, I know it's not true. So do the police."

Tammy closed her eyes briefly. "I was driving. I only told the cops that she was because I was scared. I lost control of the car when I came down the hill—" She broke off as Harold Mercer, gray-faced with worry, approached them.

"I got through to Tessa's parents," he announced quickly. "They're flying up later tonight."

"Can they get a flight out that soon?" Doreen asked. "I thought the movie location was out in the countryside."

"Rick Diamante, one of the stars of the movie, keeps a plane at a private airstrip down there," Harold explained. "He's flying them up to the Santa Barbara airport. I'm meeting them there early tomorrow morning. It'll take that long for them to get up here."

"Oh, my God, they must be out of their minds with worry." Doreen ran a hand through her immaculate hair, mussing it up and making it stand straight up on her head. "I hope to God she's not still unconscious by the time they get here."

"Mrs. Mercer," a young man with horn-rim glasses and dressed in hospital greens interrupted them. "I'm Dr. Caldararo."

"How is she?" Doreen asked quickly. "Has she

woken up? Is she going to be all right? Can I see her now?''

He shook his head. "I'm afraid she's still unconscious."

Doreen's hand flew to her mouth, her eyes flooded with tears. "How bad is it?"

"We don't know yet," Dr. Caldararo said gravely. "We're still doing tests."

He tossed around a few technical terms that Tammy had only heard on TV and then went back to his patient. But despite the long, scientific words the doctor used, Tammy knew what he meant. Tessa was still unconscious. Not responsive. And the longer she stayed that way, the more dangerous it would be for her.

No one said it, but she knew what the doctor meant.

"Tessa's in a coma, isn't she?" Tammy asked. Her eyes filled with tears and her heart thundered against her chest. Fear flooded her body. Her knees began to shake and her hands started to tremble. "She could die."

"Now, now, dear." Doreen patted her daughter awkwardly on the back. "No one's said anything like that. . . ."

"They don't have too," Tammy sobbed. "But it's bad, real bad. And it's all my fault."

"It was an accident, honey," Doreen protested. "Accidents happen all the time. Even if you were driving, it wasn't your fault."

"Of course it was," Tammy cried. "If I hadn't

been drinking, I wouldn't have lost control of the car.''

Early-morning sunlight slanted in through the blinds on the hospital window, bathing the room in a pale rosy glow. Tammy stared at the silent figure lying under the sheet on the bed.

Tessa's face was pale, almost as white as the bandage that covered the ugly gash on her forehead. Her eyes were closed, her lips bloodless and pale. An IV was attached to her arm. From the corridor, Tammy could hear the rumble of the carts and the footsteps of nurses and orderlies.

But in here, all was quiet.

Silent.

Deathly still.

"Please wake up." Tammy took her sister's hand. Her flesh was warm to the touch. "Please, please, wake up," she pleaded. She'd spent the night sitting by her sister's bedside. She'd watched, prayed, and hoped. But Tessa hadn't stirred.

Along about four A.M. she'd started to plead with God to make her sister wake up, then she'd begged, and finally she'd bargained. She told Him He could take away everything she had—her clothes, her car, her money, even her boyfriend—if only He'd make Tessa wake up. But God apparently had His own designs.

Tessa was still unconscious.

Tammy knew that wasn't a good sign. She stroked her sister's hand and let the tears roll down her cheeks. More than anything, she wanted to see her sister again. She wanted to sit around shooting the breeze, she wanted to go shopping at the mall and pretend they were the fashion police, she wanted to listen to Tessa's funny stories about her parents, but most of all, she just wanted her alive. Even if Tessa hated her, she wouldn't care. If only she lived.

"Tessa," she said softly. "If you'll wake up, I'll do anything you want. Anything."

Tessa didn't stir.

Tammy took a deep breath. Whether Tessa could hear her or not, there was something she had to say to her. "Last night, I told my parents everything. About the drinking, about how the accident was my fault. You'd be real proud of me. I told them the truth, the whole truth and nothing but. . . ." She faltered as another sob racked her. "They were really pissed. I mean, really pissed. Harold turned so red I thought he was going to explode and Doreen actually started yelling. But I didn't lie, Tessa. I told the truth. For the first time in years I told the truth about myself."

Tessa's eyes remained closed.

"Look, damn it," Tammy exclaimed, "you've got to wake up. You're not doing either of us any good by staying in a coma. How can I become a better person if I don't have you around?" She brushed at the tears that were falling on Tessa's sheets. "I mean, that's what you are, you know, a good person. Probably the best person I've ever met. I mean, look at the way I've treated you. Heck, that would have sent most people heading for the hills. But not you. You cared enough to stick around and keep trying to help me. I knew what you and Alex were doing. I knew you'd made up your mind to quit covering for my drinking. And I promise you, Tessa, if you'll just wake up I'll never take another drop. I swear it. I'm going into rehab. Honestly.'' She grabbed a tissue from the table next to the bed and blew her nose. "Doreen's even agreed to come to counseling with me," Tammy continued, her voice a broken, harsh whisper. "Like I said, they were mad, but in the end, they want what's best for me.... Oh God, please wake up, please wake up, Tessa. I can't stand the thought of this world without you.'' Tammy started as a hand fell on her shoulder. Swiping at her tears, she turned and found Doreen standing behind her. "Oh, I didn't know you were here.''

"She's my daughter,'' Doreen replied softly. "I've been here all night. I didn't want to intrude. The doctor said Tessa might respond to the sound of a familiar voice.'' She laughed sadly. "Let's face it, your voice is more familiar to her than mine.''

For the first time in her life Tammy looked at her mother as a person. She saw the torment in Doreen's eyes and the lines of worry bracketing her mouth. "She's going to be okay, Mom,'' she said gently, wanting to ease the pain in her mother's face. "I know she is.''

Doreen smiled. "I hope so, honey. Now that she's come into our lives, I don't want to lose her again. Why don't you go home and get some rest? And make Alex go too. Both of you are exhausted."

"Alex is still here?"

"Uh-huh; he refuses to leave until he knows she's going to be okay. But both of you need to get some rest. Go home. I'll call if there's any change."

Tammy shook her head. "I'll go out in the lobby and lie down for a few minutes. But I'm not leaving until I know she's going to wake up. Is Harold out there with Alex?"

"Harold's gone to pick up Tessa's parents. They should be here soon."

Tammy gave her sleeping sister one last glance, nodded, and went out to the waiting room.

Doreen sat down in the chair Tammy had just vacated. Like Tammy, she reached for Tessa's hand. "The doctor says we're supposed to keep talking to you," she murmured, "but I don't know if I've got anything to say that you'll want to hear."

Tessa slept on.

Doreen sighed. "I know you probably think I'm pretty worthless as a parent, but I want you to know there hasn't been a day of my life that I haven't thought about you."

Tears sprang into her eyes and she didn't bother to wipe them away. "I love you, Tessa. I always have. From the moment I put you in that social worker's arms and watched her take you away to give to someone else, I've loved you. I've won-

dered about how you were doing and grieved over
the fact that I couldn't keep you.'' She laughed
softly at herself, knowing that if Tessa were con-
scious and listening, she wouldn't believe a word
of it. Doreen wouldn't blame her. ''It's true,'' she
insisted, even though no one was giving her an argument. ''I know I haven't been much of a parent
this summer, either. But only because I was scared
. . . I was afraid to reach out to you, I was afraid
you'd hate me because of what I'd had to do.'' She
swallowed the lump in her throat. ''Maybe you'll
understand when you wake up. It's not as though
I've been a very good parent to Tammy. I did my
best, but I was too blind and stupid to see that she
had a serious problem. She drinks. My seventeen-
year-old daughter's an alcoholic and it's my fault.
But you've got to understand, Tessa, I did the best
I could.'' Her voice wavered, but she wasn't
through with what she had to say. ''I thought I was
doing the right thing, I thought that by giving
Tammy the best—a fine home, clothes, a car—that
I was giving her what she needed. But I was wrong.
She needed me. And I wasn't there for her, just
like I wasn't there for you.''

Tessa's eyes stayed closed.

''You know,'' Doreen continued, ''every year
Harold and I would give Tammy a big birthday
party.'' Her tears splashed on Tessa's pillow, stain-
ing the white material with fat drops of grief and
pain. ''And every time we had that party, I'd have
to sneak away and cry because it was your birthday, too, and you were gone.''

She reached over and gently stroked Tessa's cheek. "But you couldn't know that, could you? You were far away from me and living with people who loved you very much. Forgive me, honey, forgive me for what I had to do seventeen years ago. But it was the only way to save your life."

Alex was slumped down in one of the waiting-room chairs. His eyes were closed, his clothes rumpled, and his hair mussed. Tammy approached him warily, wondering if he would even speak to her. But she would make him talk to her; more important, she'd make him listen.

There was something she had to say to him. Through the long vigil by her sister's bedside, she'd faced some really ugly truths about herself. She was selfish, self-centered, petty, and sometimes downright mean. But as she'd sat terrified, staring at her sister's pale face through the endless night, she'd realized something else. She was worth saving. Tessa had taught her that.

Why else would Tessa have struggled so hard to help her face her drinking problem? Why else would she have put up with Tammy's silent treatment, cold shoulder, threats, and spitefulness. Tessa could have taken off. From the way she talked about her own parents, one phone call would have been enough to have her on the next plane to Mexico.

But Tessa hadn't run. She'd stayed to try to help her. And if someone like Tessa thought she was worth fighting for, then Tammy wasn't going to throw in the towel now. No matter how hard it was, she was going to face what she'd done and try her best to make amends.

Alex's eyes opened as she walked across the carpet. The expression on his face was so hopeful that she almost cried.

"She's still unconscious," she said softly.

Disappointed, he slumped back in the seat. "Damn." He rubbed his hand over his face. "I was hoping you had some good news. Her being out so long isn't good, is it?"

"No, it's not." Tammy refused to give in to despair. She had to stay positive. She had to have hope. Tessa was the last person who'd give up without a fight. "But she'll wake up. She's going to be fine, Alex. I just know it."

"Geez, I hope so." He started to get up.

"Sit down," Tammy said firmly. "I've got to talk to you."

Alex gave her a quizzical look, but did as she asked. "What about?"

"About us, about this summer, about you and Tessa."

"Do you really think this is the time or the place?" he asked sarcastically. "In case you haven't noticed, your sister's in a coma."

"And it's my fault." Tammy held up a hand. "But this is important. It's not about me, Alex, it's about Tessa. It's about everything I've learned from having her here. She's not afraid to talk things out. She's not afraid to tell the truth. She's not afraid to face life head-on.'' She paused and took a deep breath. ''And neither am I.''

He cocked his head to one side. ''Go on.''

''It's important to me to clear things up once and for all.'' She brushed a lock of hair off her face. ''I learned that much from Tessa. Clear the air, get things out in the open.'' She laughed softly. ''And I want to tell you that I know what you and Tessa were trying to do.''

''You mean with the drinking?''

She nodded eagerly. ''You were trying to save my life, and fool that I was, I was fighting you every inch of the way. But that's all over now, I've faced the fact that I've got a problem. I'm going into rehab.''

''Just like that?''

''Just like that,'' she repeated. ''I told Harold and Doreen everything last night. They were really mad, but they believed me.''

''Too bad they didn't believe Tessa,'' Alex pointed out. ''Maybe if your mother had listened to her, she wouldn't be lying in a coma right now.''

Tammy winced at his brutal honesty. But she couldn't disagree with him. Things might have been very different if Doreen had taken action then instead of waiting for tragedy to strike. ''I think she'll regret that the rest of her life,'' Tammy said, remembering the haunted expression on her mother's face. ''But she knows now. She's even agreed to go to counseling with me.''

Alex stared at her a long moment. ''I guess confession really is good for the soul,'' he finally said.

"Look, I don't mean to be hard about this. I guess it was tough on you having to face your parents and tell them the truth, but I'm all out of sympathy. It's been a lousy night, and it's not over yet. It won't be over until Tessa wakes up."

He wasn't trying to hurt her, but right now all he could think of was the girl lying so still in that hospital bed.

Tammy smiled wanly. She could understand what he was going through, she was going through it, too. Everyone was scared for Tessa. She'd never seen Alex so upset. Obviously, he cared about Tessa in a way he'd never cared for her.

Deep inside, she knew that she'd lost Alex forever. He'd probably still want to be friends, but she was out of the running as a girlfriend. She was surprised that she didn't mind. Alex had always felt more like a brother to her than a boyfriend. A flash of shame shot through her as she remembered that it was her hysterics yesterday that had put Tessa in a coma. Her hysterics and her drinking, she corrected silently. But she wasn't an idiot, she could learn from her mistakes. "I'm not looking for sympathy," she said honestly.

"Then what are you looking for?" he asked wearily. "For me to wave a magical wand and clean up the mess? I'm sorry, Tammy, this is one mess I can't do anything about."

"I know." Tammy sighed deeply. "None of us can. All we can do is wait and pray. But I promise you, if she regains consciousness—"

"*When* she regains consciousness," he interrupted, his voice harsh.

"When she wakes up," Tammy corrected, "and I know she will, then I'm going to tell her how sorry I am and how much I love her. I only hope she'll forgive me."

"She will," he said, his expression softening. "Sorry if I sound like a bear with a burr up its butt, but I'm so worried about Tessa, I can't think straight. Why doesn't she wake up? What if she never wakes up?"

"She'll wake up," Tammy said quickly, and put her arm around his shoulders. "She has to. You have to believe that, you have to be strong for her. We can't lose her now. God wouldn't be that cruel."

"I hope you're right." He drew a deep breath into his lungs and closed his eyes briefly. Then he shifted to pull her close. "I guess falling apart isn't going to do her any good."

Alex cradled her against his chest, but it was the embrace of a friend seeking comfort. Tammy burrowed close and put her head on his shoulder. She needed comfort, too.

After a few moments they drew apart.

"I'll go see if there's been any change," he said, getting to his feet.

Tammy got up, too. "I'll come with you."

Doreen was still sitting by Tessa's bed. She glanced up and gave them a sad smile.

"No change?" Alex asked.

"Not yet—" She broke off as the door flew

open and a slender blond woman, a taller, dark-haired man wearing thick glasses, and Harold Mercer stepped inside.

"Where is she? Where's my baby?" Lorna Prescott demanded. Her gaze went immediately to the figure on the bed. "Oh my God, she's still unconscious."

"This is my wife, Doreen Mercer," Harold said quickly, "and this is our daughter, Tammy, and her friend Alex."

Lorna barely acknowledged the introductions. She hurried over to the bed and stared down at her daughter.

"Hello," the man said quietly, but his gaze, too, was on the bed. "I'm Chuck Prescott."

Doreen stepped away from Tessa to make way for the newcomers.

Tammy stared at Tessa's parents. She'd have known Lorna Prescott anywhere. Her face had graced dozens of television shows and half a dozen movies. She wasn't a big star, but seeing a familiar TV face in the flesh was enough of a shock to have Tammy's mouth gaping open.

Neither of the Prescotts paid any attention to anything but their daughter. Tammy's heart went out to them when she saw Lorna's eyes fill with tears as she took Tessa's hand.

"Maybe I'd better wait outside," Alex murmured in her ear. He quietly headed for the door, pausing once to look back at Tessa.

"I'm so sorry we had to meet under these circumstances," Doreen said, directing her comment to the Prescotts.

Chuck nodded. "Where's the doctor? I'd like to talk to him as soon as I've had a few moments with my daughter."

"He'll be in this morning," Doreen replied. "There isn't any extensive damage, at least not as far as they can tell. But they're waiting for her to regain consciousness before they do any more tests."

"Oh, my darling." Lorna leaned down and kissed Tessa's cheek. "Mommy's here now, sweetheart. Everything's going to be all right. But you've got to wake up now."

"Daddy's here, too," Chuck said. From behind his glasses, he blinked hard to hold back the tears.

"We'll be out in the waiting room." Doreen waved at Tammy and Harold to join her. "You probably want a few minutes alone with Tessa."

At the door, she turned. "The doctor says that it's important to keep talking to her. Maybe a familiar voice will bring her out of it."

Lorna looked helplessly at her husband.

"Go on, honey," Chuck prodded. "Let her know you're here."

Lorna swallowed hard and leaned close to her daughter's ear. "Tessa, it's Mom. I'm here now and everything's going to be just fine. You've got to wake up now—" She broke off and drew in a long, deep sob.

Tessa didn't stir.

"Hey, kiddo." Chuck leaned over Tessa's pillow. "We've really missed you this summer. Next time, I don't care if we're shooting in Timbuktu, you're coming with us. Come on now, wake up. You're scaring your Mom and me. You win, honey. So you'd better wake up and get your prize."

Lorna swiped at the tears rolling down her cheeks. "I knew we shouldn't have let her come here for the summer," she said to Chuck. "I knew we should have taken her with us to Mexico."

"Now, honey," Chuck protested. "We both agreed it would be good for Tessa to meet her birth mother and sister." He patted his wife's hand and then turned back to Tessa. "Wakey, wakey, swee-tie," he singsonged, using the same phrase he'd used to get Tessa up for school when she was little. "It's time to rise and shine."

"Come on, baby," Lorna said, her voice desperate. "Open your eyes. We're here. You've got to wake up. . . . you've got to wake up—" She broke off as a sob racked her body.

"It'll be okay," Chuck said to his distraught wife, though he was having a hard time staying calm himself. "Falling apart isn't going to do Tessa any good at all."

"This is all our fault," Lorna moaned. "If we'd taken her to Mexico, she wouldn't have been—" She gasped as she felt Tessa's hand move against her fingers. "Chuck, she moved. Her fingers moved."

"Are you sure it wasn't just you squeezing her

hand?'' Chuck asked, glancing down at their en-
twined fingers.

"Wait," Lorna exclaimed, her gaze flying to her
daughter's face. "I'm not imagining it, she's
squeezing my fingers." She bent so close that her
mouth was only an inch from Tessa's ear. "Wake
up, honey," she said in a loud, firm tone. "You've
got to wake up."

Suddenly Tessa moaned softly.

"She's coming to," Lorna cried excitedly.
"She's coming out of it."

Chuck bent close to her other ear. "Tessa, swee-
tie," he ordered, "wake up and talk to us. Come
on now, you can't sleep the day away."

Tessa's eyes slowly opened. She blinked hazily
as she focused on the familiar faces of her parents.
"Mom? Dad? Is it really you? I thought I was
dreaming."

CHAPTER
TEN

Dear Diary,

Whew! They finally let me out of that place. For a few minutes there this morning, I thought Mom and Dad were going to insist on seeing the X rays themselves. Poor Dr. Caldararo didn't know what hit him when Mom and Dad started in with the questions. But finally, everyone decided I wasn't at death's door and they released me. Not that hospitals are prisons or anything, but they're not exactly a fun place to spend your summer. I was lucky, though, I was only there a couple of days.

Mom and Dad are back at the hotel and I'm here at the Mercer house. I'm not exactly sure what's going to happen next. I've got a feeling that I'm not going to be staying here much longer, but no one's said anything yet. I'm supposed to take it easy for a few days, so I know my parents aren't

*going to toss me on the first plane for Mexico.
The medical facilities aren't the best in the world
down there, so until Mom is convinced there
won't be any aftershocks from the accident, I
guess I'll be here. Not that there's anything wrong
with me. After I woke up or came out of the coma
or whatever the heck I was in, they did a bunch
of tests on me and didn't find any cracks in my
skull or loose bits and pieces floating around. But
I had a real doozy of a headache for a few hours.*

Tessa frowned at the words she'd just written and
closed her diary. She'd been home from the hospital for hours now and no one had told her what
was going to happen. She didn't know whether to
start packing or what. Her parents had dropped her
off here with a cheerful wave and told her they'd
be back later. Tammy and Doreen were both out
and Harold was at work. Alex wasn't around either.

She started as she heard footsteps in the hall.
She'd just swung her legs off the bed when there
was a soft knock on her door. "Come in," she
called.

A hesitant smile on her face, Tammy stuck her
head inside. "Hi, you feeling up to some company?"

"Sure." Tessa scooted back on the bed. "I was
wondering where everyone was."

Tammy's smile widened. "Doreen and I went to
the counseling center. We had our first session today."

"So you really meant it?" Tessa asked excitedly. "You're in rehab?"

"Of course I meant it." Tammy plopped down on the foot of the bed. "Why? Did you think I'd back out?"

"Not exactly," Tessa admitted honestly. "But I thought maybe you were just telling me about going to counseling to make me feel better."

Tammy shook her head. "No way. Like I told you yesterday, I've learned my lesson the hard way. No more boozing for me. For God's sake, my drinking almost killed you."

"You didn't almost kill me," Tessa said quickly, not wanting her sister to have that burden of guilt hanging over her head. "It was an accident."

"An accident that I caused," Tammy shot back. "Stop being so nice, Tessa. It was my fault and I'm taking the responsibility for it. That's one of the first steps, you know. Taking responsibility."

"Okay." Tessa grinned at her sister. "But if my taking a crack on the head got you into rehab, then it was worth it."

Tammy shuddered. "Don't say that. You could have really been hurt or worse. Nothing's worth that. But I think things are going to work out. Like I told you yesterday, it'll be hard, but I'm determined to kick this thing."

"Can you stop just like that?" Tessa asked. She was more curious than anything else. It wasn't that she didn't believe her sister was sincere, she did. But addictions were tough to overcome.

"If I have help." Tammy shrugged. "That's what the counseling and all that's going to do. Give me the help I need to face my problems so I don't go crawling into a bottle again."

Tessa smiled broadly. "You'll do it. I know you will and I'll help in any way that I can."

Tammy reached over and patted her sister's arm. "You already have helped," she insisted. "But I'll take all the support I can get."

They looked at one another with understanding. Yesterday, Tammy had come to the hospital and begged Tessa's forgiveness for the accident and for a lot of other things. There'd been tears, lots of them. But after they'd talked, there'd also been a new understanding and respect. When Tammy had started to cry because she was so grateful that Tessa didn't hate her and was going to forgive her, Tessa had told her bluntly that that was what family did. They forgave each other. And the girls were family now.

"Uh, I thought you ought to know that Alex and I had a long talk," Tammy continued.

Tessa stiffened. Alex was the one issue she and Tammy hadn't talked about yesterday. "And?"

"And we've now officially broken up." Tammy smiled brightly.

Tessa searched her sister's face. She wanted to make sure that Tammy really wasn't upset over losing Alex. If their positions were reversed and Alex was leaving her for Tammy, she'd be going bonkers. But her sister was perfectly calm. Her eyes were clear and direct, her smile sincere, and there was no telltale tension in her body as she relaxed on the end of the bed.

"Are you okay with it?" Tessa finally asked.

"Of course I'm okay with it," Tammy insisted. "Alex and I are more like brother and sister than boyfriend and girlfriend."

"But you've gone together so long," Tessa interrupted.

"Yeah, and now it's time to let go," Tammy said. "Besides, he's crazy about you. I'll always have a special place for him in my heart, but he's not the love of my life. It's time to move on. For both of us. So go for it, girl. He's all yours."

"Let's just hope that he knows that." Tessa laughed. "I haven't seen him except for a few minutes at the hospital yesterday."

"Take my word for it, you'll see him," Tammy replied. "But this is a family thing and Alex is sensitive to stuff like that. I'm pretty sure he's backing off now so we can get a few things straightened out."

"Straightened out?" Confused, Tessa cocked her head to one side. "Exactly what is going on here? I'm okay, right? What more is there to straighten out?"

"Well . . ." Tammy hesitated. "I think your parents want you to leave and go back to Mexico with them. I overheard them talking to Doreen and Harold. To put it mildly, they weren't exactly happy campers."

"Oh rats," Tessa muttered. "Do they know you were drinking when we had the accident?"

"Uh-huh. From the way your dad was yelling, they seem to think you'd be better off in Mexico with them. But I don't want you to go, Tessa. Do you think it would do any good if I talked to your folks? Do you think they'd believe I'm not ever going to drink again?"

Knowing her parents, Tessa didn't think so. But she didn't want to say so to Tammy. She didn't want to dash the hope she saw in her sister's eyes. But oddly enough, Tessa wasn't all that upset at the thought of going back with them. Sure, she'd miss Tammy and Alex, but there was one part of her that had really missed her folks. "Uh, I don't know."

Tammy looked at her speculatively. "Don't try to con me, Tessa. You do know. They're not going to let you stay, are they?"

"Probably not," Tessa admitted. "It's not that they wouldn't believe I'd be okay here," she explained. "It's just that . . . that . . ."

"That they want you with them because they came so close to losing you," Tammy finished. "It's okay, I understand."

"Look, even if I do go to Mexico, that doesn't mean we can't be together. L.A. isn't that far away," Tessa said earnestly. "You can come spend weekends with me and I'll come up here to visit. You'll see—we'll see each other all the time."

"You're right." Tammy smiled and stood up. "Like you said, we're family now. Besides, maybe it would be better if you do go."

"Gee, thanks."

"Don't be so sensitive," Tammy said. "But you've got to admit, with Doreen and me in counseling together, this isn't going to be a very happy place to hang out. Speaking of which, Doreen said she wanted to talk to you."

"Have her come on up," Tessa replied. She hoped she wasn't in for more tears from her birth mother. Doreen had almost flooded her hospital room yesterday. Strange, too, because Tessa would have bet her last nickel that the woman didn't have a working tear duct in her head.

"Okay." Tammy stretched and yawned. "I'll tell Doreen you're awake and then I think I'll go take a nap—" She broke off and laughed as she saw the look of dismay spreading across Tessa's face. "Don't worry," she said quickly, "I mean a real nap. With you being in the hospital, I haven't gotten much sleep lately."

Relieved, Tessa grinned. "You had me going there for a minute, kid. Okay, catch you later."

She settled back against the pillows and stared at the ceiling. What could Doreen want to talk to her about? Tessa hoped she wasn't going to ask her to stay on. Frankly, as much as she'd miss Tammy and Alex, the thought of staying in the House of Usher for the rest of the summer sent chills up her spine. She knew that part of her own reaction was due to the fact that she'd had a close call. But she didn't care. She wanted to go home. To her real home.

And that was anywhere her parents were.

She wanted to listen to her father's tirades about

the idiots in Washington and his nagging about staying out of the sun. She wanted to go shopping with her mother and hear all the latest gossip about who was doing what to whom on the movie shoot. She wanted to be coddled, fussed over, and generally driven nuts by the two people she loved more than anything.

Chuck and Lorna Prescott. Her parents.

"May I come in, dear?" Doreen stuck her head in the door and smiled timidly.

"Sure." Tessa forced herself to smile back. "It's your house."

"I'd like to think you think of it as home, too," Doreen said lightly.

Tessa was surprised by that statement, but she deliberately kept a bland smile on her face as she watched Doreen perch carefully on the end of the bed.

Tessa could see that this whole situation had taken a toll on Doreen Mercer. Her face was pale, her hair, which was usually immaculate, looked like it hadn't been combed in days, and her face looked positively haggard. She'd aged ten years in a few days. Tessa felt sorry for her.

"This summer's been fun," Tessa said hesitantly. "And I'll always be glad I had the chance to get to know you and Tammy."

Doreen raised her eyebrows. "You're very sweet, Tessa. But let's face it, we haven't gotten to know each other. I was too busy running around from one stupid committee meeting to another to take the time or the trouble to get close to you. I bitterly regret that.''

Tessa didn't know what to say. ''Uh, look, uh—''

Doreen waved her hands impatiently. ''You don't have to try and think of something to say to make me feel better. There aren't enough words in the English language for that. I had a second chance with you this summer and, as we used to say back in the sixties, I blew it big time.''

Oh God, Tessa thought, this was going to be worse than she'd imagined. Doreen was really on a bad guilt trip. ''Look,'' she began earnestly, ''I'm sure you did the best you could—''

''Nonsense,'' Doreen interrupted. ''A cocker spaniel would have done a better job of getting close to you than I did.''

''You weren't that bad,'' Tessa tried again. There was no point in making Doreen suffer. She'd suffered enough in the past few days for a lifetime. ''You were just busy, that's all.''

Doreen laughed bitterly. ''Busy? Oh yes, I was busy. I've been busy for the past seventeen years.'' She sighed. ''Oh hell, this isn't going at all like I hoped it would.''

Tessa's eyes widened. She didn't think that Doreen even knew words like ''hell.''

''I've got something to say to you and I want you to listen to me with an open mind and . . . I know I've no right to ask it of you, but I'd like you to listen with a forgiving heart as well.''

Forgiving? Tessa wondered if everyone around

here thought she was Mother Teresa. What was there to forgive? Doreen was paying for whatever mistakes she'd made in her life. "Uh, okay," Tessa mumbled as Doreen stared at her with a hopeful expression on her face.

"Thank you, dear." Doreen took a deep breath. "Let me start at the beginning," she began softly. "I think it's important that you understand."

"Understand what?"

"Everything." Doreen smiled sadly. "Why I gave you away. Why I was such a bad mother to Tammy. Why I closed my eyes to what was going on right under my nose." She stopped and stared out the window.

"Go on," Tessa prompted.

"I told you that when I found myself pregnant, I'd decided to keep my child."

Tessa winced inwardly. That was one conversation she'd never forget. "Yeah, then you had twins and I cried a lot and was sick or something."

Doreen frowned. "Is that how I explained it?"

Tessa nodded.

"That's only the bare bones of the story"—Doreen clasped her hands together—"and I probably didn't explain even that part very well. Let me tell you what really happened."

Mystified, Tessa simply waited for her to go on.

"Things were really bad for me," Doreen said softly. "I wasn't expecting twins. But when I had them, God, I was so proud, so happy. It was like Christmas and your birthday all rolled into one."

"That's not the way it sounded when you told

me before," Tessa mumbled. "You made it sound like a disaster."

"I know," Doreen admitted. "But all these years, I've had to live with the fact that I had to give one of my precious babies away...." She swallowed convulsively. "And the only way I could do that, the only way to make it bearable, was to remember only the misery of that time and not the joy. I wouldn't let myself remember how much I loved you, how much I wanted to keep you." She swiped at a tear that rolled down her face.

Tessa felt tears spring into her own eyes, but she blinked them back. "Go on."

"I was planning on keeping both of you," Doreen said. "But then you got sick."

"What do you mean, sick?" Tessa asked. "Did I have something seriously wrong?"

Doreen slowly shook her head. "Pneumonia. Your lungs hadn't developed as well as Tammy's. They had to put you in an incubator. The doctors told me that you'd need extensive medical care for one, maybe even two years." She closed her eyes briefly. "But even then I wanted to keep you. But I couldn't. You see, it wasn't just that I didn't have the money for medicine or doctors or hospitals. You needed nursing care. You needed a mother that would be home with you twenty-four hours a day. I couldn't do that. I had to work. I didn't have any choice. My family completely disowned me when I got pregnant and the man who fathered you took off. I was completely and utterly alone."

"But what about state or county aid?" Tessa asked. "Couldn't you qualify for that?"

"I could have," Doreen admitted. She closed her eyes and shook her head in disgust. "But at the time I thought I couldn't. I'd been raised by strict, hardworking people who took pride in never depending on anyone but themselves. I thought I had to be that way, too. I was too stupid, too proud to go that route. I wish now that I had. Anyway, what's done is done. I realized that if I tried to keep you, there was a good chance you'd die. And I couldn't bear that thought. I'd do anything to make sure you had a chance to live, a chance to stay alive . . . so I agreed to let you be adopted."

Tessa swallowed the lump in her throat. Now she knew. She'd been given away so she could have a chance to live.

A chance at life.

That teeny, tiny voice in the back of her head, the one that occasionally whispered in her ear that there was something wrong with her . . . that she was damaged goods or second best—it was gone. Banished forever by the truth.

"So now you know," Doreen said. "I'm not proud of myself, but at the time I thought I was making the right decision. I wanted you to live."

Tessa said nothing for a long moment. Then she leaned down and impulsively put her hand on Doreen's clasped fingers. "You asked me to listen with a forgiving heart," she said. "But as far as I can see, there's nothing to forgive. I've had a good, happy life."

Doreen stared at the small hand covering her own and then looked up at Tessa. "Thank you," she whispered. "Thank you for understanding and not hating me."

"I could never hate you." Tessa settled back against the pillows.

"Maybe it's a good thing I gave you up." Doreen sniffed and wiped at her cheeks. "I haven't done such a hot job of raising Tammy. But I felt so guilty, so unworthy of being anyone's mother. It was just easier to give her lots of material things and pretend that that was all she needed. Life was so hard when she was a baby."

"You haven't done so bad," Tessa said. "Tammy's a pretty decent person. She just needs a little help, that's all. When did you marry Harold?"

"When Tammy was two." Doreen finally brought herself under control. "I was so grateful that he wanted to marry me. I felt so unworthy of being a parent that I guess one part of me decided to devote myself to being the perfect corporate wife. Well, that's going to change now. I think Harold's in for a few surprises. But he's a good man. He can handle it. In his own way, he loves Tammy very much."

"I'm sure he does." Tessa smiled. "And life tends to give us all a few surprises every now and again. But there is one thing I want to ask, and please, tell me the truth, even if you think I won't like the answer." She plunged ahead without giving Doreen time to answer. "Tammy told me she was the one who wanted me to come for the summer.''

Doreen looked at her for a moment and then laughed. ''That's nonsense. I wanted you to come. I've waited years to see you. I know I didn't act like it, but it's true. I was the one that contacted your parents. I wrote them through the adoptees' rights agency last year.''

Tessa grinned. ''Good, it's nice to know you wanted to see me. To be honest, thinking I was brought up here to satisfy Tammy's curiosity kind of hurt.''

''Well, that wasn't the case at all.'' Doreen cleared her throat. ''Your parents are rather upset. Not that I blame them, of course. But they said they'd leave it up to you whether or not you wanted to stay for the rest of the summer or go back to Mexico with them.''

Tessa wasn't just surprised, she was downright stunned. Her parents were going to leave this decision to her? She couldn't believe it!

''Tammy and I both want you to stay,'' Doreen continued. ''But we'll understand if you want to go.''

''I'm not sure yet,'' Tessa replied. After listening to Doreen, she wasn't sure what to do. ''Where are they?''

''Back at the hotel. They said they'd be by at six to pick you up for dinner.''

Alex came by later that afternoon. He poked his head in the room and grinned broadly. ''Hey, sleeping beauty, got a few minutes for a hopeful frog?''

Tessa laughed. ''You've got your fairy tales mixed up, but come on in anyway.''

''How you feeling?'' he asked.

Tessa, who was fully dressed and lying on top of the spread, watched as he, like Tammy and Doreen, plopped down on the foot of her bed. ''Pretty good. I haven't moved around too much today because it gives me a headache. But the doctor says that should fade in a day or two.''

He nodded and then stared out the window. ''Uh, I hear you're going to Mexico with your parents.''

Tessa hadn't decided yet. ''I don't know, Alex. Would it bother you if I did?''

''Bother me? Yeah, I'd like you to hang around until September, but like I told you the other day, it wouldn't be the end of the world.'' He looked at her. ''Would it? I mean, even if you go, we'd still be—'' He broke off and blushed a bright red.

Tessa thought he looked awfully cute. ''Together,'' she finished for him.

He nodded.

''You haven't changed your mind about going to school at UCLA, have you?'' she asked. There were some things a girl had to know before she rushed into a decision.

''No way.''

''Then it wouldn't make any difference at all.''

He grinned broadly. ''Good.''

They spent another hour together making dates and going over all the things they wanted to do together once Alex was in Los Angeles. Then they talked about her sister. "Do you think Tammy will be all right?" he asked.

"I hope so," Tessa said seriously. "But like you said, it's up to her now. We've done all we can."

"Let's just hope she stays in counseling."

"Her and Doreen," Tessa added. "Funny, but it could turn out that Tammy's bout with booze will be the thing that really brings those two together."

By six o'clock, Tessa was dressed and downstairs waiting for her parents. For once, all the Mercers were home and in the dining room eating a meal together. Tessa heard a car pull up out front. Peeking out the window, she called a quick good-bye to everyone and hurried out the front door.

Her father was climbing out of the rental car as she came dashing down the driveway. "Hey, honey," he yelled. "Slow down, the doctor said you weren't supposed to exert yourself."

"I'm starving," Tessa called, delighted to hear his familiar voice, even if he was nagging. She climbed into the backseat. "Hi, Mom," she said, leaning up to peck her mother's cheek. "You look great."

"So do you, sweetheart," Lorna turned in the seat and smiled at her. "How are you feeling? Did you get plenty of rest today? You know you're not supposed to overdo it."

"I was in bed most of the afternoon," she said cheerfully. "And I feel great."

"We won't be out too late," Chuck said as he

started the engine. "We don't want to tire you out."

They chatted on the short drive to the restaurant. On the surface, everything was just fine. But Tessa could hear a note of tension in her mother's voice, and when she glanced at her father as they were getting out of the car in the restaurant parking lot, she noticed the haunted expression in his eyes. She wondered what was wrong. What were they not telling her? It would be just like them to try to keep things from her, especially as she'd just gotten out of the hospital.

Tessa didn't say anything until they were seated in a big, comfy booth and the waiter had come and taken their orders. She'd just handed her menu to the man when she happened to see her parents exchanging a worried glance. This was too much. What was going on?

"What's up?" Tessa asked as soon as they were alone.

Lorna threw a quick, guilty look at her husband and then smiled innocently at her daughter. "What do you mean, honey?"

Her mother might be a good actress, but that smile didn't fool Tessa for one minute. "I mean, you've been acting weird since you picked me up," she replied. "And I know it isn't about my health, either. I heard you talking to the doctor today and there's nothing wrong with me."

"Now, sweetie pie," her father said, and pushed his glasses farther up his nose, a sure sign that he was anxious about something, "you're imagining things. Your mom and I are acting like we always act. There's nothing wrong. You've had a terrible experience, honey. It's made you super-sensitive.''

Tessa eyed him warily. Maybe it was her imagination. Then she saw her mother poking at her cuticle with the tip of a long fingernail and Tessa knew. "I'm not imagining anything." She pointed at her mother's hands. "You never pick at your nails unless you're nervous. What's wrong? You're scaring me to death. Is one of you sick? Have you lost the part? What?''

Lorna looked at her husband, who sighed heavily. "Okay," Chuck said, "if you must know, your mother and I are little concerned about something. But it's nothing serious.''

"If it's not serious, then why won't you tell me?''

"We were just wondering what you'd decided to do, that's all," Lorna blurted.

Chuck frowned at her. "I thought we'd agreed not to put any pressure on her. This has got to be Tessa's choice.''

"I'm not putting pressure on her," Lorna said defensively. "I didn't want her worrying that we were unemployed or on our deathbeds.''

"Pressure on me about what?" Tessa asked.

"About whether or not you're coming back with us or staying here with them," Chuck replied.

"But I thought the plan was for me to stay the summer," Tessa said quietly.

Lorna smiled, but the smile didn't quite reach her eyes. "It was, honey. But after the, uh, accident, we thought you might want to come to Mexico with us.''

"Now, Lorna," Chuck said hastily. "Let's make it clear we'll understand if she decides to stay. After all, Doreen Mercer is her mother and Tammy's her twin sister."

It took a moment to sink in, but when it did, Tessa was dumbstruck. Her parents were scared. They were afraid she was going to blithely ignore seventeen years of devotion, nagging, lavish affection, and unconditional love and go off to find her roots with the Mercers. Geez, she thought, how dumb could they be?

"Doreen's not my mother," Tessa announced firmly, looking at Lorna. "She's the woman who gave birth to me. You're my mother."

Lorna broke into a radiant smile, and this time it reached her eyes. "Thank you, sweetheart. I'm glad you feel that way."

"And you're my father," Tessa said to Chuck. "You always will be. You're the one that was always there for me, and nothing will ever, ever change that."

"Oh, honey," Chuck blustered. "I know that."

But from the relieved expression on his face, Tessa could see that he'd needed reassurance.

"So what are you going to do?" Lorna asked.

"Do you even have to ask? You're my folks. I've been hurt, I've been in the hospital. I want to be babied and waited on and taken care of." She paused dramatically. "I'm going with you to Mexico."